# RUBBLE

A NOVEL

SERAJ ASSI

PM PRESS

ISBN: 979-8-88744-194-8 (paperback)
ISBN: 979-8-88744-208-2 (ebook)
Library of Congress Control Number: 2026933799

Cover by Roger Peet at justseeds.org/artist/rogerpeet and on Instagram at @toosphexy
Interior design by Jonathan Rowland

10 9 8 7 6 5 4 3 2 1

PM Press
PO Box 23912
Oakland, CA 94623
www.pmpress.org

Printed in the USA.

*To the children of Gaza;*
*may they rise from the rubble.*

I have been under rubble for one day. Or maybe two. Perhaps more. I'm not quite sure. The pain must've clouded my recollection. Time has ceased to exist. And space too. I live mainly in the spaces of my mind, which are vast and limitless.

I feel besieged, stranded in an unbending hole, a grave, a coffin the exact shape of my body. To be more exact, I had to adjust my body to this tomb-like thing, mainly by adapting to a fetal position, which explains the excruciating pain I'm enduring at the moment.

Sometimes the random bombing shakes off the rubble and helps me adjust my position.

It's a nightmare, waking up to find yourself buried underground, damp and soaked in blood, smothered under a large heap of rubble, bleeding still, breathing dust, dying alone in this subterranean pit, not a light, hardly a sound, nearly blinded, startled, trembling in fear, crying in claustrophobic pain, left to perish of horror.

It's quite dark here, except at sunrise, when the sun beams down, seeps through the rocks, and strokes my battered skin—a sign of life. Sometimes the sun kisses the rain in the sky and a faint rainbow oozes into my grave, and I take it as the sign of my salvation.

I was a child crazy about rainbows. They were colorful toys hanging in the sky. I still chase them in my dreams, whenever I sail into one of my dark reveries, which seem to abound here. Excuse my nostalgic outbursts. Glued in my fetal position, I feel like I've retreated to the womb. I see my mother in the throes of childbirth, her chest rising and sinking with her heavy breathing, screaming with joy as I kick inside her womb like a prisoner banging on the bars, ready to spring into life, keen on the freedom I've never had. I see a little tender thing, wrapped in a white blanket, gasping his first breaths while stirring to life, gazing on the world for the first time through his baffled, sleepy eyes, little knowing of life and all the madness and evil that await. They say we look at the world once, as children. The rest is memory. And now this memory is weighing on me like a gravestone.

*

Night waxes so dark even the little rainbow has vanished. Perhaps there was no rainbow. Perhaps the whole thing is a mirage of my parched imagination. The truth is that I'm thirsty, and for long, interminable hours, I see nothing but clouds sailing into my dying vision like white moons over the dark horizon. I live by the false promise of rain, and false rainbows, and false visions.

I'm tired and worn out. I'm hungry besides. I haven't eaten for days. I look a bare skeleton, a slim frame thinning out to the bones, wasting away, looking half the man I was. But it's better thus. The more weight I lose, the roomier my grave.

I'm a rabid claustrophobe. I've never trusted an elevator in my life—imagine a hole in the earth! My worst nightmare was to find myself in a wooden box nailed shut forever, thrust out of sight into a hole in the ground, left to rot and feed the worms. I never imagined, not even in my worst nightmares, that one day I would end up stranded under rubble with no way out. But you know the strange thing? It's not as bad as I imagined, especially when death rumbles on the surface and the rubble becomes my safe haven from the hell above.

The first hours were torture, let me admit. But then my body slowly adapted, and my mind started to relax. It's like being in a tight grave that only grows more comfortable over time. I tried to fight it at first, but I quickly gave up and accepted my doom. My Samsonian bravado proved more laughable than heroic. I punched out rocks and squeezed slightly through cracks in the fallen debris, but soon enough I hit a wall, in every sense of the word, and embraced my lot. I figured I should spare every last ounce of energy to keep breathing. Besides, I have no fight left in me. Merely breathing is triumph enough.

*

Sometimes I feel like screaming, to let the world know I'm still here. But I'm too ashamed to scream for help, because there are children stranded in the vicinity, and I fear that my screams could eclipse their cries for help. As far as life is concerned, children always come first. Wars hit the little ones the hardest, and for all their resilience, they are the least fit to survive. I was a child once, you know.

There's still a child in me. Stranded under rubble, I feel like a little being who's waiting to be born. You pine for your parents, especially at night, when you grow lonely and burst out weeping. Time heals, but it does not make you forget. Who will weep for me when I die? Who will sing my song? Sometimes my late father visits me in my dreams, but he never stays the night. Mother would visit if she could, but her knees are acting up. Even in Heaven we are haunted with pain.

Life under rubble resembles an incomplete death. You exist in a dreamlike haze, dazed in an existential limbo, drifting in a dreamless mist like a child in a recurring nightmare. You swoon as if you were dying and fall as the dead fall. Now and then you manage a faint stir of the body, but only to remind yourself that you're still alive. Sometimes I burst out crying with nameless joy at still being alive.

*

The war noises keep me company. Tanks crawling over the ground. Jets buzzing overhead, ready to bombard. Bombs dropping nearby, as if there were anything left to bomb in this land of rubble. Choked with dust, it resembles a body that has decomposed save for the bones.

I hear human voices in the near distance, fading echoes and dimmed booms, but they come down muffled and diminished. I hear drilling. Shouts of victory, and wails of defeat. I can smell death in the air.

There's nothing to see here, save for human remains faintly scattered in my line of sight. Children's clothes, necklaces, hair clips, combs—all torn and bloodstained. Some belongings are still eerily alive in the rubble. Broken clocks, still ticking. Music boxes, singing. Paper kites with broken spines, shifting ghostlike. Children's toys, squeaking. Dolls lying dismembered beside their slain owners. Broken toys, and broken clocks, and broken bones. Shattered windows, and broken doors. Broken hearts, and broken promises. Whole lives, whole memories and dreams have been erased, disappearing like sand in the wind, without so much as a trace.

It's funny to think that I never had a toy in all my born days. I created my own toys, mostly from rubbish. I was a kid infatuated with the dump, my wonderland, where I spent endless hours playing, rummaging, hunting for treasures, which never turned up. My best toys I crafted from fallen rocket parts and unexploded bombs. Holes and craters created by bombs were my swimming pools, playgrounds, and hiding places. My favorite hangout was a wrecked airplane, a war leftover, which lay abandoned on the roadside like a permanent landmark.

One thought terrifies me more than the others: What if this mortal place with no hope of rescue becomes my grave? It's mortifying to think that I could be buried alive, that I could witness my own burial.

*

Being under rubble is a strange thing, for there comes a time when the act of breathing becomes your only indication that you are still alive. But you are not deluded, for you know that you're living on borrowed time, and that you're clinging to life not for the sake of living, but to defy death. Just because you're breathing doesn't mean you're alive. You might as well be dead, like a dead tree stirring in the wind. You're a ghost, and your homeland is but a ghostland.

Losing one's homeland unfolds like a bad dream. You sit in your seaside window gazing out into the streets, teeming with life, bustling with people and little children. A great celestial power hits the place, and you wake up from your reverie to find yourself gazing on a vast sea of wreckage. No, you are not gazing on it, for you are buried deep underneath it—it's the rubble that's gazing down on you.

But you know the funny part? When you're under it, you don't have to see it. What sight is more agonizing than a homeland reduced to rubble?

*

I might be dead, but I'm not unalive to the human miseries unfolding overhead. I smell blood everywhere. It could be mine, or other people's. I'm not sure. It's hard to trust your senses in the dark.

I smell dust, taste dust, and breathe dust, mixed with human blood. From dust I came, and to dust I have returned, though I believe humans were created not from dust, but from the rubble of higher and nobler civilizations. Perhaps it's not a belief, merely a vision. Once upon a time, a very long time ago, humans did not know war. Sure, they would fight now and then, but they fought mainly for sport. They had no planes, or rockets, or bombs—merely bows and arrows, which caused no ruins, and hardly ever scratched the surface.

Come to think of it, I have spent my whole life under rubble. War has made us a nation of moles, hobbits, little people haunting the dead grounds and clinging to the surface of the earth like mortal things. I have seen more rubble than I knew existed. It's part of the landscape. I'm starting to believe that God created the world from rubble. Perhaps it's not a belief, merely a reckoning.

*

When despair takes hold, I indulge in hopeful visions. I hear some faraway people live in wood houses, made of trees. Surely wood would be kinder to us than broken stone and brick. It's quite primordial, living in trees. My ancient ancestors lived in trees. I was conceived in a tree, so to speak. My parents were poor and humble, and all they could afford was austere romance. Legend had it that he'd made her a wedding bed out of a dead olive tree. Nothing more romantic can be imagined.

When I was ten, my father built me a small tree house. Many nights I slept there. When war broke that year, the tree house was hit, and the roof collapsed to the ground, but I survived, for there was no rubble.

When the guns fall silent and the dust of war settles, I will marry my sweetheart and build us a wooden house made of native olive trees. We can build a little boat and sail wherever the wind takes us. I see us in a freer land, a dreamland, a never-never land, a borderless land where people roam free under the azure sky. A land without rubble.

*

There's no escaping the rubble. It's like fate: Once it has taken hold of you and had you in its grip, it becomes impossible to dislodge. This is hard to believe, coming from a dying survivor, but I'm starting to feel one with the rubble. It's like an overly affectionate mother who holds you in her tight squeeze, not so tight as to smother you, but tight enough to keep you in her grasp.

All my life I have dreamed of escape. It started as a fantasy. It was wartime—always wartime—and I watched the stars, waiting for a sign, an omen, a herald, a flying carpet, a spaceship, to beam me away. Far off in the distance, I spotted a dim light like a distant star. It was red-blue, made of sun and sky, and my feet burned to set out for it. It shone where the sky touched the sea on the horizon. Beyond the horizon was darkness, and beyond the darkness the free world.

I can still see that dim red light. It flashes through the gloom, and as suddenly fades away. Perhaps it's the blood in my eyes. Or maybe the residue of a bad dream. I can't be sure. Only death is certain. You can't trust your eyes under rubble, where nothing but dust breathes.

I wonder if the outside world remembers us, or knows about our existence. Hello, world! Can you hear us down here?

*

I have always mused about the outside world. I have dreamed of it, fantasized about it, roamed it in my free imagination. It must be an interesting place, an exciting place. Quite sure it's a safer place.

Perhaps when the dust settles and the siege is lifted, when the rubble clears and my grave is discovered, I will embark on a long trip and discover the world from east to west, go out there and suck out the marrow of life, the good free life the world is hiding from us. It's sad to live and die cooped up in one spot when there is a wonderful world out there waiting to be seen. It's a tad claustrophobic, if you ask me.

Here I am now, stranded under rubble, with no way out, and no hope of escape, except maybe through death—the ultimate escape.

In hindsight, it was a tad delusional of me to imagine that the free world could be within reach. It was laughable to think that I could coax reality into my little fantasy. There was no escaping the siege, and I knew it. The siege is our destiny, and there is no escaping one's destiny. As our wise men say, there's no hope of escaping the prison without crushing the gates on ourselves.

The best we can do is seal our grievances in a bottle and cast them into the open sea.

*

When fear takes hold of me, I burst into silent singing. I started this habit the day the war broke out. I never imagined that the war would drag on so long, or that I would survive this far. I'm still reeling from my wounds, and I sing mainly to remind myself not to die.

Singing lends death a new kind of terror, for no matter how fast you sing, death paces faster. Your soul is in a hurry, your heart is bleeding, and your feet are burning to go, but words are still burning out of you as if from a fireplace. My voice trembles some, but it lifts my spirits.

Sometimes, when I close my eyes and drift away, I see myself in a better place, a freer place, a peaceful place where war is a distant memory. I feel like I've been raised from the dead, resurrected yet still in pain, as if my saving angels had forgotten to remove the nails. You remember how lucky you are to be alive and safely resurrected when you look down and see beneath you the last vestiges of a planet now dead, where nothing stirs but the dying breaths of hapless humans clinging to the surface of the earth. Or perhaps I'm dead and all these horrors are just a bad dream. Wake me up when this nightmare ends!

*

Sometimes, when I drift off, I dream that I've been abducted by aliens and beamed away from this doomed world. Perhaps it's not a dream, merely a fantasy. Whenever I drift into that dream, I see all the loved ones I've lost in the war gathered in Heaven, awaiting my arrival. It's easy to believe in Heaven when you live in Hell. Perhaps it's not a belief, merely a wish. If there is no Heaven, we must invent one, if only to comfort the oppressed who live and die waiting for justice and happiness on this earth. Perhaps Heaven is just a vision, a desire so strong it has acquired the status of faith, though if God meant to interfere in our grinding misery, He would've done so by now. As my faithful people say: If there is a Heaven, God bless; otherwise, you have escaped this hell, and that's heaven enough.

I might be hallucinating, but these thoughts let me fly. They shield me from reality, especially when the screams around me become too loud to bear. Dreaming helps me cope. It's become my only freedom in this dark maw of white rubble, which now threatens to be my grave.

*

There is still hope in the midst of this despair. For even as I lie here bleeding, screaming with dying breaths, my mind is free. In my imagination I can envision a better future, free and happy. When the bombs fall silent and the dust settles, life will bloom again. For the past has passed, and the present is flying as we speak; only the future is certain. The best of history, we say, comes tomorrow. The present may have its horrors, but the future shall burn brighter.

It might be a surprise to you, coming from a man under rubble, but we are visionary people. Even in our darkest moment, we can see the future, and quite vividly so. It's one of our many gifts.

We are not as naive as we sound. We have hope for the future because it's all we have left. We are futuristic by nature; it's how we endure interminable indignity. We see the world through the prism of the stars, the moon and the sun, the chances of rain, the prospects of harvest, the heralds of spring. We read omens in the sky as if they were holy writ. If the heavens comply with our predictions, we say we are following our stars. Or we die waiting; then no harm done. We fold up our prayer mats, embrace our lot, and toil on without grumbling.

I remember my grandmother poring over my palm to divine my future, though, like most old refugees, she lived mainly in the past. She felt at home in it. She had a key of return, which sat on her chest for many years and waited. A beautiful old key meant to unlock the past. She always dreamed of the journey home—the day when her children would return to the dear old homeland and avenge her decades-long dispossession. She died dreaming.

She never foresaw this wholesome destruction, though she was right about the rubble, which is why she lived her whole life in a tent.

*

I cling firmly to my right to live and survive. For you must know that I'm not alone here. Grandmother is with me in spirit, and what better time to summon her hauntingly brave spirit than now?

She was a stout refugee who persisted and stood fast, and she never broke, no matter what. She endured, without a single complaint, years of grinding poverty and privation. She survived many wars and invasions. She always smelled of the soil, and sweat was her only other perfume. She was a sturdy, earthy woman, with deep wrinkles older than the land she resembled. She was older than the Strip itself. Her aspects were geological, her face ancient, her eyes deep and hollowed. The wrinkles on her face resembled the bark of an old olive tree. Everything about her was old and ancient, except her eyes, which were brown, like the soil that birthed her.

She was deeply rooted in the land, born from the soil, to which she returned. I recall her sitting by her stone stove baking bread, or curling over her old millstone grinding wheat. She always sat on the floor, close to the earth she loved and resembled. I live by the memory of those distant smells, the taste of her cooking, the colors of the old land embedded in her olive skin and vivid brown eyes. She lucked out and died before this war, holding on to her last shred of dignity. Mercy on her soul. She must be in Heaven right now, having escaped this hell.

*

Someone has died. I can tell from the eerie silence left in his wake. He'd been gasping his dying breaths for hours, screaming out feebly. Then the screams faded into a constant whimper and the music stopped, and I heard him no more. Perhaps he's sleeping, dreaming up his fantastical escape in the silence of the night.

We are hopeless dreamers. We are an irredeemably romantic species—fantasists, visionaries, idealists, boundless imaginers hallucinating beyond life itself. A rich vein of optimism runs in our blood. There is no ceiling, no roof to our visions, only that vast, illimitable space that hatched our first ancestors. Our hopes get us by, our visions sustain us, and our dreams keep us standing. No matter what the future holds in store for us, we look to it with blazing eyes and burning hearts. Once a vision has taken hold and has us in its grip, it becomes impossible to dislodge. Come war or death, we never quit. Many of us die dreaming. We believe death is the beginning of a life of eternal happiness, everlasting peace, and absolute justice.

For all the grinding misery, we remain positive. Throw a siege over us, and we let our minds take wings and fly. Soon our imagination breaks loose and works magic. Fantasy is embedded in our genes. We indulge in it constantly, building castles in Heaven where beautiful angels in white gowns wait to usher us into a life of unending pleasure. We're hooked on the afterlife, which makes us fearless at the prospect of our own death. We feed our desolate hearts on promises of rivers of milk and honey. Perhaps it's the climate, or the sheer grind of life under siege, or maybe the unending war and all its miseries. We have an unwavering faith in divine justice, the notion that those who suffer on this earth will have a better life in the hereafter. We endure that way.

*

The secret to surviving under rubble is to set your imagination free and let your mind fly above the turbulences of lower existence.

We are creative and imaginative people. When our flag was banned, we embraced the watermelon, whose colors, when sliced open, represent the colors of our flag, while the seeds embody our indestructible roots. No people more symbolic can be imagined.

We are incredibly whimsical people. Where you see rubble, we see our beloved homes refusing to set us free.

The present may have its sorrows, but the future is firmly in our grip. When things go south, we navigate north. When life turns sour for us, we let the present blow its trumpets and we sail into the future. Bury us under rubble and we will scream some, manage a little whimper, close our eyes, and dream of better times to come. Believe me, having lived through the present and its horrors, tomorrow holds no terrors for us.

*

Or perhaps I can look back on happier times, let my mind fly to the free spaces of my childhood, take a trip down memory lane through the old beaten avenues of youth. Perhaps the past is all we have. Even as we speak, the present is the past. The present is fleeting, and the future is but a wild hunch, but the past lives on, like a haunting spirit.

I was a happy child. A free spirit relishing whatever freedom life under siege afforded me. A little noble savage roaming the sandy streets of the camp like an untamed child of nature.

It was always wartime, and you never knew when the next bomb was bound to hit. Life was never a sure thing, so I embraced it fully.

I remember a boy in the heedless lap of happiness. Braving the sea. Building sandcastles on the beach. Burying himself in the sand. My favorite game was called marbles: We drew a circle on the ground and knocked the marbles into it—a metaphor for life under siege.

I loved the sea, my childhood haunt, the site of my first memories. I smile at the image of my father. I remember the day he wanted to teach me how to swim like a fish in the Mediterranean, and I ventured too far out and came close to drowning. I remember the old fisherman who taught me how to row my boat against the tide and beat the winds. We caught a big fish once, and his face parted in a triumphant smile the likes of which I've never seen on a human face since. The swells were heavy; it took us two hours to reel in the fish. One day he grew tired of the siege, ventured far out to sea, and never returned. I hope he made it alive.

The memory of those days gives me a thrill, for even under rubble, I still recall with a smile the day I unmoored a boat in the old harbor and let it sail me wherever it may, and I would proceed to revel in my aimless wandering until I was discovered and brought to safe shores.

I remember with awe those proud fishermen of yesteryear, with their bucket hats and long mustaches, wearing baggy trousers and headscarves, silhouetted against nets and waves, laughing from the belly at the merest provocation. I always dreamed of being a fisherman. One day I boarded a ship, and the captain said, "Clean up the hull and follow me." I had no idea what the hull was, so I cleaned every spot on the ship, except the hull. We all laughed about it afterward. From the belly.

Life was not a paradise, but it was bearable. It was freedom in disguise, as now I'm under rubble. One ought to wind up buried underground to appreciate the simple joys of yesteryear.

*

My name is not important. To the rest of the world, I'm a faceless hobbit, a subterranean thing stranded under rubble. I believe most people here feel that way. Humans pretend not to see us, but we are here, languishing underground, and they know it. They treat us as subterraneans to deny our existence, or perhaps to dehumanize us—to show the world that we are less than human. It's easier to bury us alive that way. And the deeper they bury us, the more they believe it.

Being underground is a strange thing. It's to live in a world that both denies and dreads your existence. Humans fear us, both alive and dead—as if dry bones could harm anyone. But we look nothing like hobbits. We are more human than we let on. We are subterranean only because others refuse to allow us our place under the sun.

But we are still here, steadfast on our land, and deeply beneath it. Waiting for our portion of light on this earth. We're not mole people, or tunnel dwellers, or subterranean beings, though the war has forced us underground. We're human, all too human. We dig down and hole up, and like all people, we go under when the earth trembles and things fall apart, and come out when the sky rises. Then we bury our dead without ceremony and go about our lives.

But we are not cavemen; we live like hobbits and tunnel down so often because the earth has shrunk on us. Show us the light and we will perform miracles, and this land abounds with earthly miracles, from the river to the sea, and for all the destruction, it still retains traces of its lost beauty and former glory. You must know that this land was a beautiful mother once, the envy of all. She was a sun-kissed paradise where God and all his otherworldly promises had no purchase. It was a pleasure just to behold the beauty of the sunset upon the sea. Then war came and all that went. Humans invaded, fire flourished, and people fell, and all that was solid dwindled to debris.

*

Life in the rubble is a suspended death, a pending life held in abeyance. This might sound strange, coming from an earthbound man, but I'm not made for this rubble. I miss the earth, the dirty soil, the golden sand. I long to be out there again, standing on terra firma.

We are earthly people, made from the earth, born of the soil, which we resemble. We live on the surface, the skin of the earth, life near the bone. We sleep on the floor, for beds are a luxury here. It keeps us grounded, down to earth, closer to our roots. We eat on the floor because of the relentless shelling. When our houses shake and the walls wobble, we sit on the ground and eat our food in haste. Every meal threatens to be our Last Supper. We eat with drones and sleep with rockets, but we always rise with the sun. Bomb us in our sleep and we will still rise to Heaven. Or so we believe, for it would be insane to believe otherwise.

We are poor but dignified. We refuse charity, not out of vanity but because charity only perpetuates our suffering. We like to earn our bread by the sweat of our faces. We believe work is worship. My father was a restless farmer who graced the land with his sweat and blood. He was born from the soil, to which he returned. He never rested. God rested on the seventh day, but my old man never rested.

Stranded under rubble, I smile at the memory of my mother, shaking me awake at the bleeding dawn, to rise and shine, and outshine my foes. *Rise and shine!* But there was nothing to rise for, no prospect in sight, only gloom and desolate skies, and a land besieged. Sometimes I fancy myself rising from the ground, as did the old phoenix from its ashes, but soon the rubble crushes me down and stirs my dream awake.

*

I have lived in this strip of land all my life. I have never lived elsewhere. I have no idea what life is like elsewhere. I'm sure it's a better life. I've never left, not out of choice, but because no one leaves. It's a vast prison, a grand panopticon squashed between desert and sea. For many years, we've lived under total siege, with no way in and no way out. Even the sea is forbidden to us. We are besieged by land, air, and sea. Our links with the outside world are all severed. Our borders are sealed. In fact, we have no borders, only buffer zones, manned with soldiers, with drones and rockets buzzing night and day. A military barrier separates us from our lost homeland, which looms on the near horizon like a lost paradise. No one breaches the barrier and stays alive. One can hardly stay alive without breaching it. Breach it, if you dare, and you'll end up buried under rubble—a siege within a siege.

I lived in a tall building, which is no more. There were two hundred of us. My room had a nice seaside view. It's a shame the mighty sea was often blocked by laundry lines, but you could still hear it roar behind the curtains. I can hear it now, roaring in the distance, like a pack of mad lions. I remember the tiny old fishing boats moored to the harbor wall, tilting idly in the surf, drifting ghostly in the winds. Last I saw of them the little boats were floating on the sunny tides.

The building had a nice rooftop. I liked to sit there and ponder what the outside world was like. One virtue of being besieged is that you feel like the center of the universe.

I hope you now understand the risk I was taking by choosing to live near the coast, right on the water. They say when humans embark on wanton bloodshed, they start with the coast, for the water makes it easy to cleanse the blood and hide the crime. For some, it's a blessing. No one wishes to die before his time, but they say when tragedy unfolds and exodus ensues, those who die first will become the envy of the living, having died in their homes, with dignity and pride.

*

The building was hit with a massive bomb. Or maybe two. Perhaps even more. I'm not sure, because I was gone with the first blast. The roof collapsed, and the walls fell like columns of smoke. In an instant, the whole building was gone, along with those who lived in it.

We lay buried under rubble, some dead, others alive. In the first hour, people screamed constantly for help. I could recognize eight voices in the vicinity, which then died out rapidly—whether permanently or briefly, it was hard to tell. They could have been dead, or merely resting, waiting in silence, which seems to linger. The human voices that once graced this place have fallen into eerie silence, perhaps forever.

Ours was a noisy quarter. Neighbors quarreled over the most mundane matters, but they were family. Everyone was kin. No one was a stranger. Only the devil, we say, is a stranger. People were poor, but they refused to be miserable. Life was heavy but bearable. People could subsist on half a meal a day, and still looked content.

It was a bustling camp, swollen by refugees, but still mostly peaceful. The camp was so densely overcrowded that if you dropped a pebble from the sky, it was sure to kill someone. Many of us have died that way. Some houses had no roofs, and no walls, hardly a floor. Our building had no garden. The real garden, we liked to say, awaited us above. Gardens be damned! The moment you put a man in a garden, he sins and falls. The whole Strip, with its olive orchards and lemon groves, was our garden. Now it's all gone, a paradise lost.

*

I was born in the Beach Camp, but I have been displaced many times since. It's funny, but being under rubble with no hope of rescue, displacement suddenly seems like a sweet prospect. Roaming is good for you, my displaced father liked to say; keeps you in good shape. Funny, my old man! One could use a laugh or two in my condition. We are funny people; that's how we fool tragedy. Laughter blunts our pain. Our humor can be dark, gallows humor, but it keeps us going. Outsiders find us a tad eccentric, but we are just ordinary people living unordinary lives, and dying the most extraordinary deaths.

Our land, now in rubble, abounded in earthly miracles. I still wax nostalgic about my old family house, which was bombed and razed in the last war, along with those who lived in it. It was located near the old port in the Sands District, the jewel of the coast. The old port itself no longer exists; it was bombed and destroyed, to the last boat.

I have fond memories of my childhood house. It was old and humble, but it was home. I remember the marbled doorsteps where I crawled as a child. The old stone front, wreathed in splendid grapevines, tinged with fallen pomegranates the color of blood, dappled with an arabesque of native trees, like living relics from a prewar past. I miss the sight of those pomegranates falling to the floor as from Eden, the red juice trickling out of them and tarnishing the ground, resembling a crime scene. I remember the old pomelo tree, basking in the glory of its own shade, wallowing in gilded sunshine or silver moonlight, enduring war after war. It had a swing where I rocked as a child, and a hammock where I daydreamed. And I had grand dreams then.

I miss our olive orchard, bathing in the keen eastern sun, awaiting the rain. The olive trees, green as emeralds, older than the soil on which they stood. It's all gone now. The orchard was burned down in the last war, to starve us into submission and to erase the most vivid token of our existence on this land. Olive trees are highly venerated here. Before the war, the Strip had sprawling olive groves, thousands of acres of native beauty rolling out to the horizon, passing from generation to generation, centuries old and still rolling, but now sadly uprooted, just like the people who planted them.

I miss the lush oranges, golden and sun-beaten, sour in my mouth, sweet in my heart. And the apples, noblest of all fruits, nectar of the oppressed. And the watermelons, with their indestructible seeds.

The sweet tinge of those days remains green in my memory. Can I evoke those memories without collapsing in tears of nostalgic mirth?

*

Stranded underground with no hope of rescue, I become wistful about the green open spaces of childhood.

I remember the day I accompanied my grandfather to shepherd his flock in the fields, and he snoozed under his fig tree having entrusted the sheep to me, and as I started to count the sheep I too dozed off and veered into a world of my own creation, paddling away into my paradisial reveries while the real world slowly receded, and by the time my grandfather woke from his midday snooze the sheep had gone. The sheer memory of my grandfather, screaming in the wake of his sheep, draws a rare smile on my bleeding face.

I have a faint recollection of my late grandfather. I remember an old man leaning on his cane, wearing his traditional scarf, fiddling with worry beads. I picture him sitting quietly on his doorstep, smoking his pipe while the world around him burned to ashes.

He died in the war, and was buried unceremoniously in the ruins of his home. It was an omen, if only I could have seen it!

*

I'm still alive, in tatters, but breathing still. When my grave tightens its hold, I take a stroll down memory lane for a mouthful of fresh air. There I venture, roaming freely through the ancestral citrus fields, lined with native guavas and clementines whose pleasant windborne fragrance traveled camps away. I pause to admire my uncle's papaya tree, standing alone in a sea of lemon trees, tempting scrumpers. I greet the loquats, and the carambolas, and the peaches whose scent has never faded away. The red strawberry fields sprawling over the green landscape, resting in the native sun, resemble an impressionist painting. A gaunt little scarecrow draped in threadbare clothes stands there to scare the birds away.

I revisit the sprawling greenhouses of my childhood, which are no more. Those sun-beaten houses, lined with fragrant cucumbers and tomatoes, were my secret paradise on this earth that was diminishing daily under my feet. That's where I played my first hide-and-seek, and stole my first kiss, and sowed my first seeds.

I remember my old uncle, spraying the evergreen bushes while wearing his war mask, resembling an astronaut, or an alien. It was in his lap where I first drove a tractor. I sat there and steered the tractor deftly along the winding road, the native winds beating against my tender face. I smile at the memory of his crimson rage when he dropped his war mask beneath the tractor's speeding wheels, which flattened it to the ground. We both laughed about it afterward.

But I also remember the red spaces that were drenched with the blood of my war-torn people, as if reeling from a tomato war.

*

Life in the camps was a tolerable hell. It was a man-made hell, but we endured it. We lived for the little joys that life under siege still afforded us. I liked to whine about it, but being under rubble and nearly dead, the siege is starting to look like a sweet memory.

Our greatest joy is the sea. But for the sea, we would've long perished from despair. The sea breeze soothes our hardships. The beach provides a sanctuary from the indignities of the camps. There is an ancient seaside rock where I liked to sit to indulge my fantastical reveries and dream the hours away, watching young boys brave the waves, or little girls dip their tender feet in the water, or old men play the flute, or fishermen celebrate their catch, or young women dream of love and romance—watching life unfold and bloom from the depths of despair. O sea, site of life and death, home of the displaced! The moment I hear its roar, an endless stream of memories flows in my mind. I smile at my mother's memory, lying on the sand, reading *War and Peace*, living the one, dreaming of the other.

Sometimes I would sit on my seaside rock with an old book, not to read it, but to admire the smiling face in the photo tucked inside it. There is a woman in my life, a childhood sweetheart, a fellow refugee. My kismet, as we say. We have in common our escapist dreams, love of freedom, and unfettered madness. Our secret romance is like a love letter sealed in a bottle and cast into the sea. I promised to marry her one day. I vowed to send for her once I escaped and settled in a new land—show her the Promised Land. I picture her sitting in her window like a songbird awaiting spring, gazing toward the horizon, waiting to pack up her old life in a suitcase and steal away on a moonless night. Innocent dreams! Love is a rebellious bird indeed.

In the dead of night, her freckled face comes alive, like a vivid midsummer daydream, and with it the memory of our unfulfilled promises. Night, making all things dimly beautiful and vividly sad! I remember two souls gazing on the road, dreaming of freedom, the moon peeking timidly from behind the clouds. It's all gone now, swept under ruins that resemble the moon's surface.

The one thing that keeps me from falling apart is knowing that soon I could be rescued and reunited with the sea, and the people who once graced its bustling shores, provided they are still alive.

*

When the sea roars its mad commotion, I take refuge in the mountain. I was a kid infatuated with the mountain. It abounded in caves, caverns, and wells—my secret haunts. There was the Stairway Cave, a spooky place, dark and damp, and filled with bats. And the Dove's Well, of course, which was dug so deep into the ground it took a stone a whole minute to reach the bottom. A boy drowned in it once. He was chasing a dove around the edge and then slid down and fell to his demise. The camp summoned a diver to pull him out. I never figured that was a true story, just a ruse to keep the children away from the well. But we returned, and returned, until one day a military truck stormed in and poured cement into the well. It was a sad sight to see our beloved well gone in ruins, buried in its waters.

But I loved the mountain. I loved it with its perils and mysteries. It was on that seaside mountain where I first contemplated the meaning of life and death. Endless hours I sat there pondering the mysteries of the world, like an ancient prophet in the throes of revelation. Too often my little reveries were cut short by enemy fires, who would ultimately conquer the mountain to build a military base, now presiding over the land like a wrathful god ready to fall upon us whenever he pleases.

Our spaces are constantly shrinking, and our times increasingly perilous. There is no safe haven but Heaven, or the hell thereunder.

*

I'm still here, stranded underground, besieged by rubble. It's a siege within a siege, and it's torturesome while it lasts. Nothing living stirs, save for a pair of hapless parents searching for their child in the ruins. When darkness falls, they sit amid the rubble, and weep.

This might come as a surprise to you, coming from a subterranean, but we are tender people, riddled with emotions. We have a strong sentimental streak. We are touchy and easily stirred.

Our men never weep in your face, but when life turns sour, they too turn and weep. My father did. I know because I saw the look on his face when the soldiers razed half of his land to build a buffer zone; then they razed the other half to build a border wall. He stood there silently and watched as a fleet of wheeled crawlers tore his land apart. All was gone. Paradise lost. That land was his heart, his raison d'être, his roots, and his emblem of belonging. I shall never forget his face as he knelt on the ground and clung to the last olive tree, hanging on to it like a child with his favorite toy, before the soldiers tore him away. He was a man of the earth, born from the soil, to which he returned.

My parents were poor as winter. When God's bounties were distributed, my father was out farming. He was too poor to deny it. He toiled day and night, like a wild animal out hunting for its young.

He worked at the big farm, built on the ruins of our displaced ancestors. He never rested. God created Man and rested, but my old man never rested. He never vacationed. The real vacation, he liked to say, awaited us above. So did happiness, and justice, and peace.

My mother was poorer than a church mouse. She left us an old copy of *War and Peace*, in translation. It was her only possession in a world bent on her dispossession. She had a golden tooth, but was buried with it. She owned a sewing machine that worked magic. It clanked and rumbled tirelessly, while she sat there singing in rhythm. She sang bittersweet songs of the beautiful life she never had.

My parents routinely quarreled over meals. They told lavish stories about their suffering, endurance, and unhailed sacrifices. I inherited their poverty. I remember a boy who survived hunger by crashing funeral feasts and scavenging leftovers at weddings, who boxed his way into food lines and rummaged in garbage piles for toys.

There is no dignity in poverty. Poverty might sound cool in rich people's memoirs, but in reality, it beats you down and crushes your soul. It leaves a permanent stain on your heart, diminishes you, and limits your dreams. It haunts you like a ghost, and you want revenge. You long to murder the monster and dance on its corpse.

And even yet, I was free, and this whole land was my kingdom. This earth was mine to roam, freely, as Heaven intended. Look at me now, buried deep in rubble, marooned in time and space. Even those calls to prayer, my only indication of time, have eerily vanished.

*

Whenever my underground siege tightens its grip on me, I dream of flying. Last night I dreamed that I was rescued by aliens and beamed away from this doomed place. It was sweet while it lasted.

I wish I was an alien myself. One could transcend the present that way, elevate oneself above mere existence. One virtue of being an alien is that you are impossible to dehumanize. Of course you can still be invaded, but they can't drop bombs on you, because gravity is on your side. Besides, there is no rubble in outer space, for it's made only by humans.

There's an alienlike quality to being displaced underground. One feels like an alien lost in darkness—eternally stranded. You lose weight, and you return to Earth a tad slimmer than before.

Or perhaps it's the moonlike rubble, and the blood-drenched soil resembling the surface of Mars.

Or maybe it's because we sometimes feel out of place in our homeland. We never understand those humans who speak of alien invasions. We never invaded anyone. We are the ones being invaded: our towns, our lives, our homes, our *humanity*. We lost our homeland to human invasions. We were building our towns, working our farms, living our lives, until they came and chased us away. Unsatisfied with driving us out, they have now forced us down deep in the dark bowels of the earth, burying us underground, beneath our own rubble.

*

Nothing stirs on the ground, save for those warplanes whooshing overhead, ready to rain down on us with the latest innovations of human evil. Even under rubble, one is not safe from those bringers of death. One could be bombed twice, and buried twice. There's no threshold.

Our sky is full of planes, but we ourselves never fly. Sure, we would fly out now and then, but only in our daydreams. Our besiegers have sanctioned anything that flies above the ground, except for their rockets. Flying kites are treated as hostile objects, and children who fly them are often showered with bullets. Still we defy the ban. Last year, our besieged children gathered under the azure sky and flew some thirteen thousand kites. It was a grand spectacle, while it lasted.

The one airport we had was bombed in the last war, wiped out, leveled, buried underground like it never existed. Our last bastion of freedom was reduced to a pile of rubble. Even the harbors, our ancient gates to the outside world, were bombed out of existence, drowned in their waters. We are lucky to merely exist.

I always dream of flying free, flinging myself into the air and whirling my body through the sky. When a border wall rose from the ground of the Strip, I wore giant wings and flew over it. I traversed borders on flying carpets, pole-vaulted barriers, and climbed over walls on giant ladders. I have acquired, in my dreams, the lightness of a bird and the stealth of a stray cat. I became evasive, maneuvering, cunning. If I ever get resurrected, I hope to return in the body of a bird. Or a cat. Or at least a bat. Bats can see in the dark. Last night I found myself stranded in a kill zone, on the run, enemy soldiers in hot pursuit, the fear of imminent death kicking at my knees. I reached a bombarded house, lying in ruins with one wall still standing, and flattened myself against the wall until the soldiers and dogs ran past, and then I doubled back the way I came. I woke up in a cold sweat.

*

Whenever the siege tightens its grip, I let my mind fly. My imagination takes me wherever I please, though I can hardly pin down my desired destinations, as the outside world remains unknown to me. Sometimes I weave fantastical places of my own creation, whole landscapes full of exotic beauty. Perhaps there's a powerful truth in the old belief that poor souls travel to Heaven after they die.

Does the soul travel after death? An intriguing question to ponder, now that I'm under rubble, with endless time on my hands to ruminate. For time moves slowly here, and the slower it moves, the larger looms the end. You feel as if you are displaced in a time warp. In the day, it whizzes by. Come the night, it slows to a crawl.

It remains a mystery to me, this soul travel, which, eerily enough, has become my last hope of escape, the only path to freedom. Perhaps I could break my siege by a mere leap of the imagination; just set my mind free, and let my soul soar and fly far and beyond.

Sometimes, when my grave threatens to strangle me, I take a prophetic leap into the future. Soon I fully abandon myself to my newfound happiness, and for a brief moment I forget all about my anguish. I picture myself in the happiness of rebirth, reunited with my beloved, basking together in the sun, the sea roaring madly under our feet. There we meet again, living anew, life after death. Everything we wish comes to us as if by magic—

It's so sad that my daydream reveries are often broken short by those resumed drillings, a crescendo building to a deafening peak that promises to either rescue me or bore into me alive. It could be the sound of my salvation, or the sound of my bells tolling. Hello, world! Do you hear my blood crying out from the ground?

*

Life under rubble has stirred up my desire to fly above the surly bounds of the earth, to revive that old dream of mine, which now haunts me like an alluring mirage. One feels like a flightless bird squashed in an iron cage with no hope of escape, and I was a free bird once.

I let the drills hammer down, and I fly myself into a world of my own creation, a world filled with ethereal spaces and azure skies, with no rubble or dust, only boundless landscapes of sun-beaten moondust.

I always wanted to fly, for the sheer love of freedom, or escapism—to elevate myself above the siege. It started as a nightmare. I was a wild kid with an untamed spirit. My soul burned to fly, and the earth was shrinking beneath my restless feet. One day, I climbed a high border wall, covered my chest with feathers, strapped a pair of wings to my arms, and flung myself into the air. Carried by the wind, I glided a considerable distance, but

I had not bothered to fashion myself a tail, so I crashed horribly and nearly died. I vowed never to fly again.

There was nowhere safe to fly to, and nowhere to land. Besides, I never trusted flying things, and who can blame me? Those giant fiery birds rise from the ground like the phoenix from its ashes and pierce the sky like snorting dragons, breathing fire and spreading death and destruction. One moment you are a human being with grand dreams and hopes; the next, you are crushed under rubble like a rat.

*

I can hear the monsters whirling overhead, ready to spring on us and wreak havoc on the heedless ground.

My father believed airplanes were flying coffins. "What happens if you jump out of a doomed plane?" I asked him once, and he replied, "I suppose one dies on the way down." Funny, my old man. Haunted by his gallows humor, I vowed never to board a plane in my life. Not that the world was rolling out a red carpet for me and beckoning me to fly.

Born under siege, the only flying things I knew were magic carpets spun in my childish imagination. Or "flying" checkpoints posing as border crossings. Or fighter jets about to bombard us. Or stray drones swooping down from the clouds. Or jubilant planes parading in celebration of a recent victory. Or missiles heading inland with hypersonic speed. Or earsplitting helicopters raining down hostile leaflets. Or buzzing drones spying on us. We counted planes to help us sleep, the way other kids count sheep. In wartime, we would scurry underground and cocoon ourselves there like earthworms. We came out only when the dust of the earth had settled, like baffled soldiers emerging from a manhole in the street, believing the war was over.

Nowhere was safe, and the land was just as formidable as the sky. The one time I ventured beyond the border wall was on foot. It was quite memorable, because I met death on the road. I remember wandering for hours through unfamiliar ground, traversing hostile terrain with no life in sight, land mines, buried in the last war, lying dormant and sinister on the road, though you could feel the monsters ticking beneath your feet. Nothing stirred alive save for a batch of unsmiling soldiers perched in their watchtowers, waving me backward—to the prison. I had to zigzag my way back through a barrage of flying bullets. You should've seen me, beating the wind like a wild cat! It was freedom, in hindsight. By what miracle I survived it's hard to tell. I believe it was divine intervention. Or perhaps blind luck.

*

Sometimes, when night falls, and the inevitable darkness looms, I burst out weeping, whether from fear or sadness, I don't know.

I was a brave kid, endowed with a tameless spirit and dauntless courage, which never failed me in moments of peril. I took no small pleasure in teasing the border patrols. We played catch, hide-and-seek, and other, more bloody games. I never quite feared death in those days. It was death that feared me! My favorite game was to brave the graveyard at night. I was not afraid of the dead, for they seemed peaceful and powerless. It was the living who scared me. I had my faith to draw on then, and the inner strength to shove that monster away. I had a few brushes with mortality. I survived some close calls. They were moments of sheer horror, save for the immense existential delight that comes from suddenly realizing what it means to be alive.

Look at me now, trembling in my underground grave like a sheep penned for slaughter, shivering at the mere sound of drilling!

*

I can hear the sound of jets buzzing overhead with a cosmic rattle, ready to bombard. Those modern carriers of death never tire or retire, as if endowed with heavenly powers. You can hear the sound of our destruction approaching on the wings of doom.

I was a kid bewitched by planes. Fallen airplanes, wrecked and abandoned, were my playground. Fallen rockets were my playthings. My hideouts were holes in the ground in which these objects had once lain. My first swim was in a deep crater dug by an air strike. One hot, airless night, a stray rocket began to fall apart just as it flew over our rooftop. The thing foundered, releasing a mighty chunk of itself that came clattering through the air, landing with a tremendous bang on the narrow pathway beside our house. The ground rocked, earth splattered, the soil boiled, and the windows rattled. I could feel our old house caving in. A gaping crater had formed. People crowded around to look at the fallen object. They stood staring into the crater, holding their breath, their lips parted, eyes popping out like wild mushrooms. It was as if a star had broken up and fallen from Heaven. We filled it up with seawater, attached a slide to it, and dived in. I nearly drowned that day. To my good luck, a passing stranger glimpsed my finger raised above the water and pulled me out. For all the anguish, it was the happiest day of my life.

That was the last time I saw my war-torn people in that innocent state—spellbound with amazement at the sight of a fallen rocket. War after war, people have become so unperturbed by bombing they now treat it as they would a random rain shower. Old men eat their breakfasts, fill their pipes, walk over to the hill, and watch their homes or tents burn down. Women bake their bread in haste and eat it before it's leavened. You never know when it'll be your last meal.

*

I take solace in the sea roaring in the distance, mixing memories and desires. I like its roar, the sound of a thousand waters. I like the sound of broken waves. It's a metaphor for the siege: You feel the waves want to break through, but they are arrested by the breakwaters.

I was barely born when the siege started. Now I'm twenty. Twenty years a prisoner! It's like doing life, except that I've never killed anyone. I'm the one being killed—my youth, passed in captivity, my dreams, my hopes, my humanity. My family! My parents married young, too young, to raise a family before it was too late. It was wartime, and nothing kindles parental yearnings like war. They married too soon, and as soon they died, leaving me an orphan. I shall never start a family, for I dread the prospect of losing one.

I was a happy child, despite the childhood I never had. I remember myself in early boyhood pedaling my creaky bike through the cobbled streets, chasing girls coming home from school, saluting dusty workers heading back from the quarries, or home from the fields. My mother, sweeping our doorsteps with her old straw broom. My father, coming home tired, shaking the dust of labor off his person. My younger sister crawling, walking, growing into a gone girl. My brothers fighting each other for the thrill of it. It was a madhouse without wardens, five young spirits coming of age in the midst of all that rage.

I remember a young boy in the heat of war, chasing tanks with his slingshot, stones, and bare hands. I remember a family in the madness of war, huddled together under one roof, holding hands under the relentless bombing. That was the last time I remember us together. Seven masked faces sat sequestered in a windowless room, praying for mercy, waiting for the madness to stop. It's quite startling that any of us survived. It took seconds for our bond to be broken forever, like beads falling from a string. It takes seconds to lose everyone, but a lifetime to fathom your loss, and you never truly heal.

There's one thing worse than dying in a war, and that's being the sole survivor of a whole family. But you carry on, because life grinds on.

*

Sometimes I listen to the sea and ponder what the outside world looks like. I wonder what lies beyond the horizon. Quite sure it's a better place. I dream to swim far and away, to a freer land, a land without walls, or borders, or buffer zones, or fraught crossings. I envy the birds, flying on the wings of freedom. I envy the fish, sailing free across the waters. I smile at my father's memory; his words still echo in my head: "I will teach you how to swim in the sea like a fish!"

My father had an inherent fear of displacement. He kept a compass to help him navigate north, should things go south. I remember there was an old atlas in the old house with a map tucked in it, which he kept unfolded, as if expecting an imminent exodus. He had an old clock that kept time, and it was a good time to keep. He also kept a telescope to look out for human invaders at sea, little knowing that the new invaders were falling on us from the sky.

*

Memory blurs as to what happened. I have a vague recollection of it. I remember there was fog and great confusion. People were in total panic. Bracing for doom, families let their children sleep in different places, so that if part of the family was killed, the rest would survive. It's like a sacred tradition here. You don't live twelve wars without learning a thing or two. In the last war, whole families were wiped out in an instant. Families still wished to die together, hence they sat there waiting in a last embrace. It's not wise to die and leave the children behind in this man-made jungle. I still bear that cross.

People were expecting death at any moment. Women went to bed fully dressed, fearing, in their chaste inclination, the prospect of being discovered under the rubble in a state of immodest dress. People wished to die with dignity. It's human, all too human. Boys wrote their names on their limbs, while little girls wore name bracelets and anklets, so when their tender bodies were blown to smithereens by a smart bomb, they could be identified. Who's smarter now?

There was great scrambling and stumbling in the camps. People flocked to the border gates like frightened sheep, some carrying their belongings on donkey carts, others fleeing with nothing but a blanket and a bundle of clothes. They fled in exodus lines, leaving behind warm beds and wet clothes on the line, brewed coffee and meals uneaten, and a thousand other chores undone in the heedless haste of exile.

And all the love left unmade.

*

From the dark silhouette of my seaside view, I saw it all. I witnessed the madness unfold in vivid detail. A girl, who had visibly lost her eye in the first bombing, sat smiling in her window, staring down at the crowd through her good eye. She waved to me, pointing to the road below, as if wondering what had possessed me not to take flight. Could she see with her one beautiful eye what I had failed to foresee?

It was a mighty crowd, a thundering sea of humanity in the throes of a great flood. But it was hardly faceless. A child in a princess dress waddled through the crowd, seeming sad and inconsolable, lost in a sea of faces. Perhaps she was looking for her crown, for she sadly inspected her bare head. No one was watching over her, or holding her hand, or comforting her. No one to take her home, and maybe there was no home. Her kingdom was no more; she was lucky to have a scepter left.

There was a great hullabaloo on the road. A beautiful little girl was looking for her lost earring in the midst of all that greater loss. Perhaps she was in no hurry to be exiled. A bundled baby, who seemed hungry, was eagerly thrusting his big toe into his mouth. The imminent bombing meant nothing to him. He was not crying, merely baffled.

And it was baffling, really, to see all those people trusting their fates to the uncertainty of exile. Those children sure can see through us.

The Strip resembled a burning city in the havoc of an exodus, like chaos before creation, except there was no creation this time, only annihilation. Many accepted their doom and stayed put. Others made a mad dash for the gates, but finding them sealed, they returned to their homes and braced for Heaven's mercy. They sat in their homes, holding each other in a state of fraught silence—embracing not from fear, but lest they die apart. People want to have a stake in their destiny. You hear them say, "If we are not free to live, can we at least dictate the terms of our death?" But the Angel of Death is blind, as they say; he acts on a whim and strikes with cold hands, and you never know what misery he has wrought until he's gone.

*

What ailed me? What possessed me not to run away? Was I too gutless to take flight?

I decided to stay put, not out of bravery or martyrdom, but because I had nowhere to go. I'm not the sort of person who succumbs to fate and bows to destiny, but I want my dying place to have an address, a landmark, a memory. Is that too much to ask of fate? I wish to die on my native soil, near my parents, and brothers, and ancestors, and all the loved ones who graced this land with their blood.

I'm not a hero, far from it. If I stay put, it's only because my survival instinct tells me so. It's wrong to assume that those who escape are gutless cowards. They say when things fall apart, those who remain resign themselves to fate: death or survival, whichever comes first. But those who flee, who fold their tents on a moonless night and leave, refuse to accept their doom. It takes guts to run away, to pack your life in a suitcase and go without saying goodbye. You can never fully untether yourself from home. The world is a heartless place, and those who are rootless—who allow themselves to become rootless—have no real place in it. We refugees carry our old homes with us, like snails. Those of us who stay put and remain steadfast deserve a decent death, with a lasting address and marked grave, but only those who find the courage to uproot themselves and face the prospect of dying thousands of miles away from home deserve to live.

My worst fear is that I will perish slowly under rubble, and that by the time I'm discovered, my body will have decomposed to where there's nothing left of it to bury, merely a pile of bones without a name or identity.

*

I'm still under rubble, languishing slowly, a tiny glimmer of light stranded in a vortex of darkness, with no way out. Like a jinni trapped in a dark lamp, waiting to be released into the light. In the day, I wax hopeful. Come nighttime, my hopes are dashed like broken waves.

Any faint glimmer of hope is erased by persistent cruelty. For days, rescuers have been looking for a missing child, aged five. The child was believed to be alive, stranded in a bombed car, besieged under fire, stirring in a carful of dead bodies. Or so the rescuers hoped. For days, the whole Strip forgot about its miseries, and prayed for the child. It's our people's way to endure the madness by clinging to a fragment of hope in the heart of darkness. You overlook the unfolding tragedy to search for a faint gleam of light. Day and night, people gathered amid the rubble and prayed for the little girl.

This morning, the child was found dead, her body decayed almost beyond recognition. She was identified by a necklace she wore. Her only weapon was a crown she was wearing. Despair rumbled back.

But if you believe the age of miracles has passed, consider the story of Baby Unknown. Days old, and incredibly thin, she was found by rescuers in a tree facing her bombed home. It appears she was flung into the branches by an air strike that killed the rest of her family. Left nameless, rescuers christened her Unknown. Judging from her umbilical cord, she was a day old when she was rescued. People believe she was hidden there by an angel, hence her new name: Angel. Her story is that of thousands of wounded children with no surviving family—nameless little angels in a godless world.

Or consider this miracle, which has reached my ears as if by a divine whisper. This morning, rescuers saved a baby from the womb of her mother, who lay dying from a bomb injury. The mother's man and her other daughter died instantly, but she survived just long enough to deliver this miracle. The nameless baby lay wriggling and crying in an incubator, with a tag around her wrist that bore the name of her dead mother.

*

Death rumbles on the surface, and audibly beneath it.

There are noises of war and death in the camp. I can hear the wails of bereaved mothers, the howls of grieving fathers, the screams of newly orphaned children. I can see the face of our doom approaching on clouds of dread. I hear people, full of evil foreboding, bracing for the horrors to come, dashing everywhere and nowhere, as if trapped in a death pit. I might be blind, but I'm not without visions.

Our enemy is invisible to us, because they only strike us from the air. They're bombing the camps with relentless fury, where waves of displaced people are besieged, squashed in this enclave like sheep penned for slaughter, pounded with unguided bombs that kill in great quantity. They like to strike crowded places because it amplifies our death toll, and what victory is sweeter than seeing many of us dead? The birth and death of ordinary people leave no trace in the annals of history. To the rest of the world, our last howls are but a fart in a hurricane—a mere nuisance. Our death rarely makes the papers, and even when our slaughter finally makes the news, it's told of only in the passive voice, like an act of God, or some natural disaster.

From my rubble hole, I can hear nearby towers falling like columns of marbles. I can sense smoke billowing from the ground as if from a dragon's mouth, and there is a brief moment when I can't tell clouds apart from the smoke of war, or day from night, or life from fiction.

Even the sound of drilling, my last token of hope, has eerily vanished. Perhaps it's better thus. Perhaps I'm safer here in the rubble. Whenever the sky rages, it leans closer to me and holds me tighter.

*

A violent shiver steals over me as I ponder my fate. People are busy saving themselves, fleeing for their dear lives, or whatever remains of them. Rescuers are too scared to venture out, for the bombing has not abated one bit, and it shows no signs of abating. I wonder what it feels like to die under rubble, to perish slowly, to be buried alive, left to rot into the ground and feed the worms of the earth and the hovering vultures. There is no hope for me. There was never hope, and there is not going to be any. They say that if you survive the bombing, and escape the flying shrapnel, and dodge the snipers' bullets, and outrun the fires, and endure the cold, and outlive the diseases, and outlast hunger, then you may have a chance to live. Perhaps there is some mercy in dying in the first instant of bombing, vanishing instantaneously, in your sleep, in the midst of your dreams.

I tremble at the prospect of dying under rubble, perishing alone and undiscovered in my earthhole, my body decomposing, offering itself to the rats as rotten cheese. It's not far-fetched.

*

I'm lost in a dreamless haze, too frightened to sleep, and too tired and battered to stay awake. In my delirium of pain, I see a young woman swinging her sleepless child, rocking his little bed to the rattle of rockets, lulling him to sleep, singing, *Sleep, my sweet little bird!* She has a warm voice, softer than the rain, and calm as a midsummer breeze.

My mother was an ordinary woman living in unordinary times. I see her as a goddess, ageless in her absence, younger in my memory. She was a beautiful girl once. I know this because a vestige of that beauty was always visible in her. I can picture her in the days of her youth, washing her young feet in the Mediterranean, dreaming of marriage and romance, indulging in romantic visions of the future.

She was passionate, volatile, and quick to anger, and I stirred her rage into a froth. She was eerily peaceful in her better days. But come the war, she was like a wild bear robbed of her cubs. But she loved me, because that was all she could afford in her state of abject dispossession. It took her dying for me to be touched by the power of her affection. I do miss my mother, though I hardly remember what it's like to have one. I feel lonely without her, like a motherless cub besieged by a pack of starving lions roaring for its blood.

In the dead of night, her face comes alive, and with it the memory of all the times she sat by my bed comforting me, singing her ageless melodies. I can feel the touch of her comforting hands reaching out to me from the grave. I resist a powerful desire to weep.

*

The sea is roaring madly. I can hear the waves rise and fall beyond the breakers. I remember all the loved ones I've lost in the madness of war, and all the loved ones I'm about to lose. The loss of my homeland is abstract, a symbolic memory, a collective tragedy. But the loss of a loved one never heals, because it's a private one.

I remember my first love. It was wartime—always wartime. We sat on the old seaside rock, holding hands, our hearts swaying with the tide, the waves roaring boldly under our feet, the mouth of the bay dripping foam like the slobber of a mad dog. It was a forbidden love, in a forbidden city, but it was sweet while it lasted. She had a beautiful face, and beautiful eyes rimmed with kohl. The most beautiful eyes under the native sun. Her fairish, hennaed hair ebbed and flowed like the waves, flirting with the sea breeze, wisping into her eyes. It wound gently round her neck, fair and smooth. Her olive skin, her lovely earthy scent, her soft deep voice, her unkissed virgin breath that mixed delicately with the gentle breeze. I tried to kiss her, but she resisted. She was not quick to defeat, like the race that hatched her. Last I saw of her, she was sitting in her seaside window, combing her dark, forbidden hair, gazing out into the night. I hope she's survived, my cat with seven souls! She's too young to die. We have a life to live together, and a thousand broken promises to mend.

*

I'm still under rubble, in tatters, but alive yet. I have a bleeding wound. I feel pained and sickened. My mouth tastes of blood, my nose smells of the sour reek of death. I resist a constant urge to vomit.

The smell of blood is omnipresent. One can detect the presence of human bodies, strewn lifeless on the red ground, bombed to smithereens. It's a miracle that any of us has survived.

It's sad to think that the human faces that have graced this place are no more. I ponder the fate of my childhood pals. We had a whole life together. We were the talk of the Beach Camp, where the hustle and bustle of life roared louder than the sea and cloaked the grinding misery of the camp. We liked to play hide-and-seek, hopscotch, rebels and soldiers. Many perished in the war. Others joined the resistance, and I saw them no more. The rest are rotting in prison camps, someplace in the desert, without so much as a sign of life.

I never joined the resistance myself because I'm too fainthearted to bear arms. I can hardly wield a knife. The sight of blood nauseates me. I remember when I was a boy our old neighbor trusted me to slaughter a bird for her, and I passed out before the bird was dead. I promised my father to resist with my pen, to write and hurl my words like fiery stones. I promised my mother to stay alive.

Our land is red with sweet martyrdom. It's a crazy idea, this martyrdom, the notion of dying for something that you won't be there to witness or enjoy. It takes a great deal of sacrifice to offer yourself to the altar for a higher goal, greater than yourself, like a sacrificial lamb.

Hadn't my father sacrificed his finest lambs to please his God, who would sadly abandon us in our bleakest hour?

*

My sad reverie is cut short by the sound of a fire belt, the bombs raining down with renewed ferocity. The monsters burn like a thousand suns and erase everything under the sun. Imagine an asteroid has hit the place, wiped it off the map, and rendered it a timeless moonscape full of strange geology. Bombed it back to the Stone Age, or a prehistoric time. But who needs a cosmic disaster with these humans? Take it from a man stranded under rubble: All black holes are man-made.

I smile at my father's atlas, lying eerily open on its shelf, as if trying to whisper something in our ears, but we could not make it out.

Perhaps it's easier to kill us that way, to wipe us out from a distance, from the cold detachment of the skies, at a safe remove from the crime scene. They dub it modern warfare, but it's clearly barbaric. It's futile besides, for if they waited a bit longer, we would all die eventually. Excuse me if I laugh, but this rubble is having a delirious effect on me. It's better to die laughing than perish from despair.

Alas, it only looks barbaric when done with stones and slingshots. As our fishermen say, if you steal with a small boat, you are a pirate, but if you steal with a big ship, you are a great army.

Look around, there is a sea full of fish not far away, and we are here starving to death, rumbling with hunger! It appears the relentless bombing has scared the fish away. Who's the pirate now?

*

The enemy likes to commence their massacres in the Beach Camp because it's right on the coast. Start with the coast, they say, for the sea makes it easy to cleanse the blood. The generals like the sight of our blood, but they dread our existence, and nothing says existence like traces of our dried blood haunting the empty roads.

It was a bloodbath, to judge from the buzz and bustle of rescuers. I can hear them, shouting in loud staccato bursts, collecting the bits of dismembered bodies, as if solving a puzzle. There are other survivors; you can tell from their dying screams. The screams, so full of pain and agony, are too dreadful to bear. I suppress my pain, out of shame and guilt. In my condition, you feel lucky to have survived in one piece. You feel ashamed to be alive while many of your kind perished.

The whole place feels like a maelstrom of slaughter. You feel eerily safe under rubble, lucky to be spared the carnage overhead. You know things are falling apart when the rubble becomes your last refuge in a place on the verge of annihilation.

From the inescapable murmur above, a dystopian image emerges: Rescuers are placing the severed limbs of slain children in small cardboard boxes; they label each box with a name and body part, and bury it.

You hear babies' cries, and then silence, followed by motherly wails. You hear children screaming through excruciating pain, as if shocked to realize that being alive may not be the best of destinies. But even in the midst of unspeakable agony, you detect glimmers of hope. One boy is asking the rescuers, "Will a leg grow for me in place of the one I lost?" A girl wonders, "Can I enter Heaven with one leg?"

Sadly, the sacred books are silent on these small matters.

*

Life under rubble is a strange thing, for there come moments when your pain gets lost in the cacophony of howls and melts slowly into that sad whole. Destiny wants you to hear it all, and witness it all.

The voices sound too tender for all that pain. These children are likely too young to remember their names, or fathom the depth of their loss, or realize they have been orphaned. Some survive in tatters. Others luck out and die. Many are in limbo. There is hardly a house without a tragedy, one gathers from the unceasing wails.

One feels sorry for the little survivors, who are bound to spend their lives with missing limbs, like flowers cut too soon. Children with missing limbs, and missing parents, and hearts too tender to apprehend the pain that lurks ahead.

The camp itself no longer exists, one can tell from the mounting ruins. The place resembles a charnel house speckled with human remains. Or so one hears. Rescuers are laboring to collect the remains of children whose bodies lie scattered on the ground. I can hear a rescuer shouting, "Whose legs are these?" Raise your hand, rightful owner, should you still have one left! How tragicomic!

They say it's rare to find a full body, so people settle for remains: hand, leg, toe, piece of hair—anything they can bury. You hear of a grieving father, standing amid the rubble, holding a pair of small sandals to his chest. It's a sad sight, when you picture it; you can't bury a child's sandals and call it a grave.

Families are struggling to identify loved ones from their clothes, or shoes, or hair, or teeth. "She had a ponytail," one bewildered mother says in elaboration, though given the ubiquity of slain little girls with ponytails, I fear she needs to be more specific. It helps if the girl was wearing a crown, or a headband, or even a flower, though it's doubtful these ornamental features could survive intact.

You hear a grandfather, kissing the lifeless body of his grandchild, calling her "soul of my soul," weeping bitterly. You know it's tragic when old men burst out weeping. Our men tear up only when praying. Only women find the courage to weep. When my father's father died, it was my mother who wept. Women wailed and men elegized. She wept freely that day, the way she would weep at the end of a romantic film. She had an eerie affection for horror flicks, as if life wasn't horrific enough already!

*

The heat is unbearable. I'm bathing in a pool of my own sweat. The roaring fire in the vicinity is the sound of a thousand flames. Night becomes day, and darkness collapses into blinding light. I can hear tumbling towers close by. I hear the sound of burning trees—native trees, older than the soil in which they stood, gone in flames, like torches blazing with light. Even the fishing boats in the nearby port, if you trust the murmurs, are burning in their waters. One hears of old shops in flames. Food shops, toy shops, sweet shops. Perfume shops, for you can smell it. Native incense, fragrant and aromatic, which would usher me into the day in my better days. You hang in a fog of your morning delirium, savoring the aroma of native food wafting out of the windows. It's so delicious you feel like wolfing it from the air. The sun beams down, and you sit there unperturbed, delighting in the sight of children coming from the local bakery, loaves of bread tucked under their arms, looking happy.

I remember the one time it snowed here. It was many winters past, sometime in the heat of war. I was five, the war fifty. Dispatched to buy bread, I ventured out barefoot, from sheer force of habit, or mere childish recklessness. By the time I reached the local bakery, my tender feet were numb, my hands lifeless, my face frozen, and my nose a bloody pink as if freshly beaten. I stood there quivering, a poor refugee in a heartless winter, weeping in the wake of his windblown tent. It was the longest walk of my life. I had never imagined cold could be so bitter. Still, the snow offered a welcome respite from wartime, a breather from Hell. It was a gift from Heaven, jewels falling to Earth, casting a white shroud over a land blackened by war. It kept us warm and safe, covering the land in forgetful snow. I felt pure, unstained joy as I ventured home, the loaf of bread tucked under my arm, the snow adding a sugary crest to my head. Innocent times.

It hasn't snowed since, though snow would do this bleak place good.

Life was a delight then—the morning breeze, and morning coffee, the first whiffs of cardamom flying out of the windows. Our people live for coffee; that's why we rarely sleep. The magical aroma creates the illusion of a new day, a new beginning, a new hope.

*

The familiar smell of dead animals is horrendous. An army of flies is hovering overhead. You can tell there is a donkey, blown to bits, lying wounded somewhere nearby. You can hear the poor ass writhing in pain, braying through its dying breaths, the vultures circling over it. You hear the normally silent lambs, bleating sadly, choking, dying a death of indescribable agony. I smile at the memory of my childish innocence. It was a holiday, and my father was about to sacrifice a lamb to please his God, and I dashed into the scene screaming, pleading with my baffled father to spare the poor animal. Innocent times.

The enemy spares no one. You can hear soldiers taking potshots at the sheep for sport. The poor animals have done nothing to warrant this cruelty, but the banality of evil is too boundless to contemplate.

You hear shots, and silence. Shots, and silence. It seems the soldiers are shooting anything that breathes, and when they find nothing breathing, they shoot into the air. They seem more terrified than they let on, visibly incensed, screaming constantly, shooting with mad fury at anything moving. A fallen tree leaf would provoke an unceasing hail of bullets. These magic machines never run out of fire, or tire of shooting. They are made to kill in quantity.

Even the little scarecrows have been shot on their crosses!

*

The familiar patterns of exile resume. On the main road, children have loaded the corpses of their loved ones on donkey carts and wagons, and headed for exile. I hear a boy, a breathless boy. He has loaded his baby brother in a wheelbarrow, which he shoves with great effort through the mud, under heavy rain and relentless bombardment.

My first ride was on a donkey. A distant memory draws a rare smile on my battered face. Our camp had a small zoo here. To amuse the children, the zoo crew painted a donkey with black and white stripes, to pass it for a zebra. The children seemed happy, but the poor ass looked rather depressed. Animals have rights here, mind you, even when the people themselves are treated as subhumans.

Nowhere is safe. North or south, death looms everywhere. Geography has ceased to exist. People run from one death to a more certain death. They move south, and finding it twice as deadly, they return north to die in the rubble of their homes. There they sit, over my grave, spinning their tales of horror like the owls of yore. Few have escaped the maw of death. This morning, bracing for the storm, seventy people boarded a fleeing convoy headed south. Moments later, a bomb hit the wagon with chilling precision, killing everyone on board.

The story has sent shocks of horror down the Strip's spine. I remember, on hearing it, a violent shiver sweeping down *my* spine. It's sweeping still, blowing within like a thousand winds. It gives me chills to think that my sweetheart was on that wagon.

I smile at the memory of two tender souls, riding a horse-drawn wagon through the rolling green hills of youth, blowing dandelion flowers into the wind to make wishes, the sea roaring in the distance, the sun shining down in its full splendor.

*

Death rumbles through the land, and the one thereunder. The desire to live gives way to the wish to die decently. But whenever I ponder my inevitable fate, the howls of children nearby dwarf my trepidation.

Frightened children are weeping for escape. Perhaps they have seen their dead parents eaten by animals in the streets, and they fear a similar fate. I can hear a little girl, sitting alone amid the rubble, stroking her cat, pleading with it not to eat her after she dies. The animals are not to blame. They act on instinct, though some animals seem more humane than those who call themselves humans. Animals have a great affinity with the people here. They seem sad to see the people go. They lie by their bodies in a mourning state. They bid farewells to the dead, console the wounded, and follow the displaced on the path of exile, chasing and clinging to the little children as they head for the unknown. They seem not to fathom what's happening, which is a blessing, when you think about it.

I think of the little girl, still stroking her cat with trembling tenderness, and it's at this frightful moment when I remember that I lost track of my cat in the midst of turmoil. Last I saw her was moments before Armageddon. I sat stroking her, and she moaned and let me know that it was time for her milk. Perhaps she was trying to whisper something in my ear, but I could not make it out for the thunder of jets. She could sense danger in the air. Cats are masters of survival; they have that foreboding instinct that never lies. She was a stray little cat, and I adopted her in the last war to spare her the horrors of the streets. Little knowing of the horrors that awaited us underground.

My mind drifts to my furry companion. The fearful expression on her face, a premonition of imminent disaster, returns to haunt me with vivid astonishment.

She was trying to warn me, but I failed to make it out in the chaos of the hour. But she will survive. Our cats have seven souls. Or so we believe. You see them rambling across the camps under relentless bombing, treading through rubble and dead bodies. They will likely outlive us, and haunt our killers like specters.

*

It unfolded like a bad dream. The cat moaned, and there was a massive blast, and the building trembled some, and then vanished into thin air. It's like a video game, except that the victims here are real. I knew them by name. I knew their dreams and hopes, which are no more.

What happened next eludes my recollection. There was a blur, and for a brief moment I went blind, and deaf, and mute, which hardly mattered, for I was speechless already. I seemed to suffer from a morbid loss of the senses. But I kept breathing, and that was triumph enough. I screamed some, and before I knew it, I was under rubble. I let out a desperate cry, but no one could hear me for the noises. For a brief hiatus, I was breathless, on the verge of passing out. My heart missed beats. I panicked some, banged on the hopeless walls, which echoed only the rattle of jets. I lay there petrified, curling up in a spasm of terror, weeping tearlessly. I tried to scream my way out, but to no avail, for my mouth was sealed with dust and every slight sound I managed to make was swallowed by my own whimpering. I was a tragicomic hero silently screaming the agony of his mad soliloquy.

In my initial delirium of pain, I fancied my sweetheart waving to me from her seaside window, to let me know she was safe. But how could she possibly survive what had killed so many, my kitten with seven souls?

*

Of the two hundred people who lived in my building, few have survived. Some are still scattered in the vicinity. The rest are likely buried under the rubble. Criers have called people by name to see if they are still alive. No answers, only echoes.

A violent shiver steals over me as I remember my childhood sweetheart. Last I saw her, she was perched in her seaside window, gazing out on the red horizon. We grew up together. We played hide-and-seek, tag, and hopscotch. I kissed her once. It was a forbidden kiss in a forbidden city. She wept, and I promised to marry her one day. She was a pretty little girl. Green eyes flecked with amber, olive skin, beautiful dark hair longer than the night, and the most tender of smiles. What has become of you, my beloved?

In the dark solitude of my grave, I weep for my sweetheart.

We subterraneans are more sentimental than we like to admit. For all the unending war and its tribulations, we remain tender people, tough as nails on the outside, but warm and soft within. We are not incapable of love.

We are more romantic than we let on. Perhaps we look a tad inhibited, but we have feelings too, though we tend to be shy in romantic matters. My father cut a dashing figure in his better days. But he was a quiet and bashful man, timid to a fault, with the devout modesty of the old prophets. He had downcast eyes, which he kept firmly lowered in the presence of women.

We are humble and chaste people. Our men sport no tattoos and wear no jewelry. Our women cover their hair, out of modesty, but they remain beautiful. Old women throw a veil over their faces, which only enhances the beauty still in their eyes.

My sweetheart had long, dark hair that touched her hips when unfurled. For modesty's sake, she plaited it beneath a black-and-white scarf and red flowers. What betrayed her beauty were those thin strands that emerged stealthily from under the scarf, spreading proudly on her shoulders, gently uncurling with the puffs of sea breeze. I remember kissing her many times before I remembered to breathe.

*

Rumor has it she was last seen on the convoy headed south, which was bombed with chilling precision, without survivors. One hears dreadful whispers overhead, like the shrieks of an owl that foretells disaster. But I refuse to believe that my childhood sweetheart, a girl so full of life and verve, is no more. The silver lining of those bombs is that they shatter beyond recognition, so if she has died in the bombing, I won't recognize her anyway, which keeps alive the delusion of hope. It's like when a body goes missing under rubble; it keeps hope alive. What do we have but hope?

She was an aspiring artist. She painted bits of native landscapes on canvases. She had a street gallery once, which sold but one painting. People who can barely afford food put no stock in art. Or perhaps they have no interest in landscapes. What good are landscapes when they acquire the status of a lost paradise? I hear artists these days are more invested in things abstract, which helps to escape reality.

Had she managed to escape south in the bleeding hours of dawn? She would be safer that way. For all its torments, exile is more desirable than death. No one who died has ever returned. But the exiled live by the hope of return. You may die waiting, but you never lose hope, for you never lose sight of the homeland. For love's sake, I hope our paths will cross again, whether here or above, whichever comes first.

*

One is lucky to be blind and deaf in this desolate hellscape bereft of life and color. You would be twice as lucky to lose your sense of smell. The landscape has the scent of scorched dust, as if it has been burned by flying dragons.

My eyes are blinded by dust, but I can see what lies beyond my sight: a wasteland of debris, dotted by deep craters where homes once lay. I see rubble everywhere. Perhaps it's the dust in my eyes. Or maybe my grave is but a miniature of a greater ruin, a destruction so colossal it resembles the remnants of an ancient civilization unearthed after lying buried for ages. I picture towers of wreckage, one hundred feet tall and still towering. I can see it all, and vividly so. I can hear it too, for walls have ears, as we say, and what is rubble but the residue of broken walls, and broken hearts, and broken dreams.

I picture a ravaged landscape, a vast horizon of dust and dirt. I see the old beaten roads of childhood, filled with the dead, and reeking of blood, and trampled by heartbroken survivors. The land, once a paradise, now sits on its own ruins, and it's ruins all the way down.

Once upon a time, a long time ago, the old people of this earth knew little beyond fetching fresh fuel for their fires. Now, the new people can burn enough fuel to whirl themselves around the globe, on their way to bomb the old people. That's human history in tragic miniature.

*

One can weave whole tales from the sad murmur of horrified survivors roaming the surface. I detect a father, trampling through the ruins, collecting bits of his child from among them. He seems in a great hurry, slowed down only by the sadness he bears in his heart like a cross. I smile at the memory of my father. He was a hoarder. He collected bits of rubbish, piles of it, for a rainy day. He did well to luck out before this war. Knowing my fainthearted father, he wouldn't have the heart to collect his son's remains from the rubble.

From the unceasing lamentations, I detect another bereaved father, holding the body of his slain child, screaming in terror. His screams echo over the surface, and audibly below it. At least he *has* a body.

Many bodies remain missing, or scattered, or buried under the rubble. For days, a man, who lost his whole family in the bombing, has been searching for them. When night falls, he sleeps alone amid the ruins where his house once stood. He strikes me as one of the living dead, a shell of his former self, but the persistence with which he pursues his search mission can only be described as superhuman. Perhaps he's waiting for the war to end, not to rejoice, but to hire an excavator to dig out his loved ones, and to bury them properly.

*

I lend my ears to a steady rumble beside me. Someone is obviously dying. You can hear the rattle of death in his voice, which dies out rapidly, and as rapidly recedes into morbid silence. You can glimpse his hand protruding from the rubble, as if pleading with us. You can smell the sour reek of death in his gory breath.

Wake up, man! Can't you hear the birds chirping? Can't you hear the drills spinning, grinding their way through the rocks?

I wish to tell him a story, to keep him alive. Or a patriotic poem, to lift his spirits. Or a native joke, to soothe his pain. Or perhaps I will stir him awake with a blaring scream, tell him rescue is on the way, hope is undead. I wish to shake him alive, shake him out of those dark throes of death into which he's drifted, show him the light on the horizon!

But he seems at peace with his destiny. Perhaps he has nothing left to live for. Perhaps he wishes to hasten his journey to Heaven. Perhaps he *is* in Heaven, smiling down on us, the earthbound.

It's not far-fetched. Sometimes I dream that I'm in Heaven too. It's sweet while it lasts, and too damn ephemeral to be Heaven.

*

Some moments are not to go unremembered. I'm speaking of the immense joy of pulling a child survivor from the rubble.

Amid the blaring chaos, a rescuer bursts into happy tears when he discovers that his own child, long missing under the rubble, is alive, visibly in tatters, but breathing still. The man is a doctor; surely he could stitch his baby back together, should he have the heart to do so.

I brace myself. Perhaps my time will come. Soon my grave will be discovered, and I shall exit into the light. But I'm in no special hurry. Children come first, remember? At least my body is still largely intact. I'm still in one piece, mainly. I must've lost a tooth or two. Perhaps more. I still have feeling in my hands and legs, though I can barely move, or bang on the walls, let alone walk. My nose is likely broken, but I can still smell, which is a curse, when you ponder it. My eyes are undamaged, mainly, but what the hell, I can't see anything anyway.

*

Some moments thrust you into a state of emotional limbo, undecided on whether to weep or smile. You hear a child, weeping quietly beside his mother's lifeless body. He seems not to understand what death is. Perhaps he thinks she's sleeping. For when a stranger offers him a piece of fruit and lends a comforting hand, he stops crying.

I remember a boy, a newly orphaned boy, hovering over a heap of lifeless bodies, gazing down into the waiting crater, weeping, wondering what colossal force had snatched his loved ones away. The house itself was gone, razed to the very foundation, with nothing left but a scar. Like a dandelion blown bare by a passing wind.

I remember my mother in the throes of grief. When my young brother drowned in the deep blue sea, I broke the bad news to her, and witnessed the first stirrings of horror on her face, a blank horror no words can express. I remember her, sitting beside his lifeless body, weeping and stroking his hair, her face white as a corpse, her eyes bleeding colorless pain. My brother drowned chasing a fish, not for sport, but because he was hungry. Never trust the calm sea.

Haunted by those memories, I cling tighter into my fetal position, as if reveling in the protective dark aura of my grave. In my hopeless desperation, I let loose a hysterical laugh, a tragic cackle by which I hope to convey my utter contempt and horror for all things human. I laugh so hard I almost forget to breathe.

*

There is a wedding nearby, being held amid the ruins. I can hear the ululations, the sound of rice scattering on the silent rocks. I can smell the incense that would usher the happy couple into marriage. Happiness still sprouts here, like wide weeds through the rocks. Sometimes the ululations grow so wild you wonder if it is a wedding or martyrdom.

It's madness. A mother loses her son; she ululates, prays to Heaven, and thanks God for the gift of martyrdom. These scenes of native resilience, known among the natives as steadfastness, have baffled outsiders and confirmed their worst prejudices: It appears that the more indifferent to death we are, the less human we seem to outsiders. Our besiegers say that believing in Heaven is a dangerous notion, because it makes us fearless in the face of death, renders us a nation of martyrs. But we believe in what we believe in.

Ululations burst out again as a man long presumed dead miraculously emerges from the rubble, noticeably diminished, but alive still, to judge from the rumors buzzing overhead. He stands there weeping, hopelessly pleading with his mystified children to recognize him.

His survival lifts my spirits and fills me with sudden joy. I would ululate if I could! I even manage a smile as the man continues to plead with the children. I remember one day I came home from school and waiting for me was a strange bearded man with thick, grizzled hair and a slight frame. Oblivious to my bewilderment, he approached me with outstretched arms, and I ran out screaming.

It was my father, home from exile.

*

Heaven has proven more generous than the earth thereunder, and for all the miracles unfolding, few survivors have turned up.

Pulling someone from the rubble is an intricate operation, for you need to dig with manual tools, like axes and crowbars, and communicate with survivors who can hardly breathe. It's a race against time and nature. Every second matters, for the voices underneath fade and vanish rapidly, like a dying echo.

Sad tales abound. A father finds himself buried under rubble together with his son; he embraces the child in a tight squeeze to protect him, little knowing that the child is dead. Nobody dares to tell him when they are found, knowing that hope alone is keeping him alive.

Sometimes, the rescuers themselves break down and collapse from emotional exhaustion. Laboring under relentless bombardment, rescuers often wait for days, sometimes weeks, before they pull the bodies from the rubble, and not quite intactly.

I wonder how long I've been buried underground. Time moves slowly here. I've lost my sense of it, hanging here with no hope of rescue, marooned in this timeless twilight with no light in sight. It could be daytime, or nightfall. I'm not sure. Time no longer exists. Or, it exists, but only as a mute harbinger of the death lurking ahead, ready to gnaw away at my stranded body with its inevitable toll.

Sometimes there is no telling dawn from sunset. But for the red blood, the place is a monochrome of dust and rubble. You feel like you are existing in a dystopian world, a ghostland, a modern city of the dead.

*

I hear a grinding sound crawling on the surface. I gather it's the sound of a bulldozer loading bodies into waiting craters. No tombs, no funerals, no eulogies. Thanks to the bombs, the craters need not be dug. They lie there waiting for the dead, like the deep abysses of Hell. Oh, the heartless crawlers! You can hear the monsters crawl over the surface, picking up the lifeless bodies with their bloody forked teeth. The mere sound of those treads makes your skin crawl!

And as you wait there quivering, a blast rumbles, *boom*, and you hear a house tumble, like a sunken ship being swallowed up. As if the earth had split and sucked it in. Even the dust left in its wake is astonishingly audible. People gather. They stand gazing down into the chasm like hovering spirits, shaking their heads in great bewilderment, swearing by the seven heavens that moments ago there was a house full of people standing in what's now emptiness.

I feel a great void in my heart, a rot in my soul. Numb with pain, my body is like an empty house, a deep dark hole, a crater. I can feel the worms of the earth vying for my remains like little vampires.

*

The hustle and bustle of collecting the dead weaves a tale of horror and lends death new terrors. People are transporting the dead in animal carts. People are driving the carts themselves, because horses and donkeys have all but perished. One can tell from the eerie silence the mighty species have left in their wake.

The dogs are acting strangely. Set free by these human horrors, they chased the soldiers through the camps, howling and assaulting them fiercely. Even the dogs can smell evil.

In revenge, the soldiers unleashed *their* dogs in the camps, mauling women and children for sport. You hear the wild beasts roving over the rubble, ready to sniff my fear.

I tremble in my grave. I have a crippling fear of dogs. When I was a child, a bemused soldier let loose his dog, which leaped at me, mauled me, and took a piece of me as a souvenir. I never truly recovered from that encounter. There I lay on the ground, writhing in pain, moaning and bleeding like a wounded pet, a warm blend of human blood and canine saliva wafting into my nose, while the soldier and dog left laughing, without so much as looking back to see if I was still alive. I can still hear that barking laughter echoing through the years.

*

If horses and donkeys have perished, imagine the fate of weaker animals, like cats. Where a house once stood, a group of orphaned children are laboring desperately to pull a cat from the rubble. The sound of a terrified cat stranded under rubble is haunting, for in its frightened state, the poor animal's sounds are spine-chilling. Its moaning cries make your skin crawl. If immortal cats with seven souls are so petrified, imagine the children!

Other children, who refuse to be orphaned, embark on rescue missions that seem rather cruel. A boy is pulling his father from the rubble with all his God-given powers, pleading with the corpse to speak to him, to give a sign of life, which never comes. With the last of his strength, he picks up a shovel, digs a grave, and buries the body without ceremony. The clanks of his shovel send violent shivers down my spine.

Another is laboring, alone, with bare hands, to pull away the fragments of his bombed family house, where his parents and siblings are buried. His quixotic mission is clearly futile, but he seems determined.

It baffles me to think, lying nearly dead and long buried under rubble, that for all the drilling and digging, no one has found out about me. Hello, world! Are you listening? Can't you see the Grim Reaper, our dark angel of death and messenger of doom, hovering overhead, lurking behind these walls, waiting in his flying casket like a winged dragon, scythe at the ready? Can't you see the vultures circling?

*

I have lost my bearings. I haven't seen the light for so long, I'm nearly blind. I smell nothing but dust and blood. I hear nothing but wails of death. I see nothing but darkness, a monochrome of a dead place. My heart is bleeding, my eyes two balls of dirt, my head burning hot, throbbing like a ticking bomb. I'm tired, depleted, worn out. My grave is closing up on me, and my body is petering out, becoming just a thin skin. I haven't eaten for days. Last I ate was a mouthful of dust and dirt, served to me by fallen debris in the initial collapse.

I feel weak and feeble. I look frail and visibly diminished. I'm cold and sick besides. I haven't showered for days. My clothes are dirty, bloodstained, and my shoes are showing holes. I'm sporting a long, unruly beard, like a mountain monk. My hair is gray with dust, crowning my head like a crust of snow. My teeth are yellowing, rotting slowly in their sockets, and I needn't see them to know their color. I stink, but no one can smell me, for the blood reeks more strongly. For a fleeting minute, the underground smelled good, but that was only when the perfume shops in the nearby market were bombed. Even the drugstores were blown up, if you trust your smell.

Nothing living stirs, save for stray dogs, and the vultures floating above. An old woman sits amid the rubble of her home knitting, to judge from the rhythm of her subdued singing. She seems to have no inkling of the tragedy unfolding about her. I gather she's deaf and blind, which is a blessing in these times. Her steadfast spirit amazes me.

I remember my mother, her frail figure bent over the sewing machine, patching my pants, singing to herself. She had a warm voice, especially in wartime, when the winds of death howled outside. The world seemed an untroubled and decent place then.

*

People have found life amid the rubble. Just now I was stirred awake by the screams of two survivors fighting over the ownership of a clothesline. I woke up in smiles, laughing in my agony.

I can make out a woman sweeping a doorstep in a room still standing. Without fuss or grumbling, she proceeds to bake a meal for her children in the midst of the rubble. It must be someone's birthday. I can hear the child pleading for candles. Who needs candles in this hellscape?

The little rascals have lost their right to be spoiled and pampered. They eat whatever comes, and settle for the few crumbs left by their starving parents in their humble sacrifices. Holidays come and go unsung.

I make out a little girl, likely orphaned, selling matches overhead, and I smile at the irony. Can't she see the whole place is ablaze with fire?

All is eerily quiet on my front, save for two old men who sit playing backgammon in the ruins, smoking like dragons, laughing and coughing in one breath, and chatting about politics, the chances of rain, and the prospects of war and peace.

I let out a desperate scream, but their laughter waxes louder.

The familiar aroma of tobacco reaches me in the solitude of my grave. I remember my late uncle. He was a war photographer. He took my first photo, which features son and father marching to stop the war. That photo has outlived time itself—twelve wars and still hanging! I remember him roaming his photo studio, bathing his prints, a cigarette dangling from his mouth, unflicked ash hanging precariously from the butt. He smoked like a restless dragon, rarely pausing for breath. He coughed often, incessantly, until one day the music stopped. He died in the last war. He died with the evidence; a bullet pierced his camera, and rested near his heart. Nothing remained of him. Hardly a photo.

I remember my grandfather, puffing his pipe while the world burned. He spent his dying hours praying, a belated reckoning with death. Bless his faithful soul! On his deathbed, he asked me to quit smoking, to live long and witness peace in the land. Amen to that!

There they are, dead and gone, resting in peace at last.

*

Within earshot, a group of young men sit comfortably on a surviving sofa, flanked by rubble and ruins, smoking. They have made pipes from bullet casings, which abound here in great plenty. When it's your land, you accept whatever fate offers you. I would join them for a smoke if I could. I'm not going to die from natural causes anyway; I might as well be dead already. Hello!

Let the men smoke. What harm can a few pipes do to a land gone up in smoke? Believe me, from my little hole in the rubble I have breathed enough smoke to keep Hell rolling.

With a heavy heart, I sit in my fetal position reminiscing over the dear homeland, now flattened beyond recognition. My melancholy mind wanders over the gray horizon, where nothing looms but the remains of a land that stands on its own ruins.

We are merry folks; it's a shame to see us go. We are kind and giving, generous to a fault. A streak of mad hospitality runs in our veins. We keep fires burning by our tents to lure in strangers. Our home is your home, we tell strangers, who sometimes take our words quite earnestly. We are hardy people. We endure and carry on. We make do and pull together. We persist and hold out. By nature, we're optimists. If half our land is destroyed, we thank Heaven for the other half. We take our pain lightly. Bomb our homes, and we will find a hole in the ruins to fill with water and bathe our children. Blow up our houses, and we will find a step amid the rubble to sit on and fill our pipes, and smoke the pain away. Destroy our land, and a new homeland—hills, olive groves, and orange trees—will bloom in the hearts of our children. We believe there is hope in despair; it keeps us going. We suffer in silence, but we never break. Exile us, and we will pitch our tents and praise God for the fresh air. We thank Heaven and carry on with our miserable lives. We survive.

Please don't forget us; remember we had a life here.

*

Today I have witnessed more horrors than I knew existed—unprecedented cruelties never seen in the annals of war. I feel years older than I was yesterday. I'm constantly sick. My face is pale with terror, my hair graying fast, and my heart dead. My eyes are blind with dust, but I can sense death like a rat before an imminent disaster.

I hear a father, holding his two children, one in either arm, both seemingly dead. He is standing over the rubble, weeping, screaming, pleading with the world to stop the madness. In his voice, I sense a history of injustice coming to a froth. It breathes with rage and sadness, which I have never heard come together in one breath before. They say grief is a noble feeling, but he is beyond grieving. It's madness—the howls of a horrified father waving the dead bodies of his slain children, shaking them madly in the desperate hope of waking them up!

I remember my father in the good old days, throwing me up in the air like a plaything, and just as soon catching me as I safely landed in his Herculean arms. I resist a sudden desire to weep.

I hear my mother's voice reaching me from the grave. Or perhaps it's a real voice—the wail of a bereaved mother lamenting a dead son. I'm too bewildered to tell. I see things, I hear voices, I fancy ghosts. There is a constant howl in my ears. I feel I am in the grip of madness.

*

Sometimes I forget that I'm buried under rubble. There is enough misery on the surface to make you forget about your own. At least I have the luxury to lament and ponder my loss, and lean on kinder times. I have an eternity on my hands to kill.

People are denied the dignity of grieving. In the bustling hub of life and death overhead, where rescuers are busy saving whatever lives they can, a mother is holding two children in her arms, one dead, one alive. She dashes about in panic, screaming, undecided whether to mourn the dead or help the living to safety.

She's hardly alone. From the murmur above, I can make out another grieving mother, who sits cradling a corpse wrapped in a white shroud. A sad sight, when you picture it. You hear of a woman, hugging a skeleton that belongs to her slain child, whose skin, you gather, likely melted away in the bombing. Or perhaps perished from hunger. "You see this skeleton?" she tells the rescuers. "It's my son."

Have you heard a child taking his last breaths? I have, and it's not a pleasant sound. Or the newborn whose first breaths now threaten to be his last? Rescuers are trying to revive a fetus inside a mother ripped apart by shrapnel. You can hear the little thing squeal, a hopeful sign of life that seems to fade rapidly. People stand there and pray for the poor little soul. It takes a miracle to save an unborn life.

It would take a river of ink to write the names of the slain children in this Golgotha of the dead. Those little souls had names and faces. They had stories, dreams, and memories. It's all gone now.

*

I'm still under rubble, languishing slowly, rotting away in this underworld, with no way out. In the day, I wax hopeful. Come nighttime, my hopes are dashed like broken waves.

Sleep eludes me. I can neither sleep nor stay awake, constantly drifting in my existential limbo, as if condemned to eternal torment. I feel restless, wary as a sleepless god, keyed up as a restive devil, undecided whether to slumber or sober up. I'm hazed within my own thoughts, drifting in a dreamless miasma like a child in a recurring nightmare. I swoon as if I were dying and fall as the dead fall. I might as well be dead. Wake me up on the Day of Judgment!

At least I have a roof overhead. Outside my grave, a family of ten, all girls, are standing in the rain, pleading for a tent. You know it's a tragedy when having a tent overhead becomes a dream.

At least the girls are unscathed, and spared the horror that ensues.

Now and then survivors will let loose a medley of unrestrained howls, and who can blame them? The rubble may have blocked the light, but one can still see the darkness in its full gloom. The bone-chilling scene runs a moment too briefly, but it's harrowing while lasts. A wild dog scampers by without a howl, cantering madly through the ruins, a dead child dangling from its mouth.

I let out a horrified scream, but there's no one here to hear it.

*

Of the recent bombing, there's nothing novel. It's the same old story of death and destruction unfettered, with new weapons.

The place reeks of death and has become a bloodbath. People with evident injuries lie in pools of blood, screaming in great agony, pleading for help, which seldom comes.

I nearly pass out. I space out quickly. I'm a rabid hemophobe, incurably squeamish. I faint at the mere sight of blood. The one time I donated blood, I passed out. Blood nauseates me. I'm feeling sick and queasy, my face turning yellow, like the flesh of a lemon. The smell of hot blood is clinging fast to my nose. But I'm alive to my good fortune. At least I'm not dead, if by death you mean the cessation of brain activity. I'm still in one piece, mainly—in emotional tatters, but otherwise intact. My body is still whole and hasn't been torn to shreds by the bomb. It's merely my heart that's bleeding.

I'm weeping. I'm not sure why. It could be my bleeding wound. Or perhaps my sad reckoning that death is not far-fetched. It's marching on certain feet. I never feared death when it loomed near. I feared it only when I contemplated it in the abstract. I dreaded the idea of it, the fact of it, the inevitable truth of it. It was a philosophical fear. But seeing the grim monster approach so near, so fast, ready to spring upon me with its eternal grip, I'm suddenly overcome with existential dread. I struggle to keep my eyes open, lest I fall asleep and bleed to death.

Sleep, my sweet little bird . . .

*

The hub of life and death overhead resumes its usual bustle. Rescuers scurry out of the shelters to save whatever can be saved. I smile with sad irony. It seems that whenever I push my luck and brace for my salvation, new victims mount up with mocking speed.

Rescuers take weeping breaks. They will stand in an empty corner and weep for five unbroken minutes. When they return, they put on brave faces and resume their facades of strength. Knowing that the wounded revere them as godlike and invulnerable, they stand fast and never break, except when unseen. If God is weeping for us, as we believe, it's only because He remains unseen.

We subterraneans rarely weep, but when tragedy hits, we weep bitterly. In the dark privacy of my grave, I weep for my people.

*

The morgues have filled up. I know because rescuers are pleading with people to bury the dead immediately, without ceremonial delays.

Tales of horror abound, to tell from the sad whispers traveling overhead. One still hears certain rumors from underground, for even under rubble, human gossip is inescapable. It's as if someone has dropped a tireless radio in the ruins and never picked it up. Mouth to mouth it travels, like a pandemic.

As hospitals come under relentless bombardment, people keep the dead bodies in food refrigerators and ice cream trucks. Disheartened, I hark back to happier days, the summers of our content: the ice cream trucks of childhood, blaring with loud music to lure in the children, who chased them through the sun-beaten streets with breathless excitement. I can still hear the tune, sounding in my ears like a bedtime lullaby, and no amount of shouting can drown out its sweet melody.

The land is shrinking on the dead. You hear of people, whole families, buried in layered mass graves with not a sliver of daylight between them.

I ponder my burial place in this vast necropolis, though I'm starting to believe that perhaps the rubble *is* my burial place. And you know the strangest thing? It's not the worst of destinies.

*

A buzzing miracle has just unfolded.

Thousands of native bees broke out of their beehives and ran riot. But instead of assaulting our people, the uncaged bees, as if divinely sent, chased and assaulted heedless soldiers with toxic stings in a stunning surprise attack. Even bees can sense evil. You should have heard them buzzing, like the sound of a thousand drones! It was a spectacular sight. My only regret is not being up there to watch it unfold.

The assault proved so vicious that enemy forces had to airlift in an entire battalion to rescue the soldiers. Vengeful planes tried to bomb the bees, but it was a futile tactic, for the impassive species proved too elusive for the bombs. It's laughable that our besiegers attempt to solve everything with bombing.

They say bees die when they sting; the little martyrs never cease to amaze. I can still hear the godsent bees humming in the distance, evoking old memories. I remember the native honey, sweet in the mouth, warm in the heart. I remember the honeybees, going from flower to flower, collecting the sweet nectar. I remember a child in the lap of happiness, chasing butterflies among the flowers. I was never afraid of bees, for they only attacked in self-defense. Innocent times.

*

In the midst of my nostalgic reverie, I hear a voice, a man's voice, a clearly distressed voice. It bears an eerie resemblance to my father's, when things fell apart and his deep, earthy tone morphed into a whimper and became too distressed to be recognized. I hear a father, desperately trying to fetch food from a garbage pile nearby. The pile has nothing decent to offer him, evidently, save for a bag of rotten potatoes, which he gladly accepts. You can feel the rot flying into your nose through the rubble. If hunger were a man, I would have slain him. I would murder the monster and dance on its corpse.

Starvation looms, on the surface and surely below it. The enemy has blocked food from entry into the besieged Strip, to starve us into submission, or perhaps condemn us to a slow, agonizing death. Children are fainting in the streets from hunger. You hear them rummage for food in garbage piles, picking through mountains of tumbledown wreckage, while rescuers stand there helpless, for nothing they can do would assuage the flaming fire inside the little ones.

People are hallucinating from hunger. You can hear the monster rumble on the surface, and audibly below it. In their hopeless deprivation, the little rascals eat whatever sparkles. You hear a child crying out, "Candy! Candy!" You manage a sad smile, a faint sigh of relief. But then a scream of agony ruptures the air, followed by a scramble of rescuers laboring to extract a rocket bolt from the child's belly.

You hear children, standing over the rubble, drawing food in the sand, and craving it. Others are drawing houses. Kites and rainbows. Blue skies. How can art flourish in this silhouette of ruins?

I hear a mother, a hapless mother, telling her starving child to hold out until the truce comes. But what does a little child know about truces, or ceasefires, or pauses, or suspensions of hostilities? Children are creatures of nature; they must be fed without suspension.

In the delirium of hunger, I sail into one of my sad reveries. I picture the food lines, queuing up in the wee hours, with no end in sight. Waves of people standing in fraught silence, holding their empty bowls, waiting for the bread that never seems to come.

We subsist on amazingly little hope. Visions of Heaven keep us going. One feels in the throes of a long, torturous fasting. Except that this hunger is not heavenly sanctioned; it's human-made.

I always fasted as a child. We fasted to satisfy God. The trick is to go hungry enough to hallucinate that you are in Heaven. One day I fancied that God was my chef. It was a delicious dream while it lasted. My mother cooked delicious food. I regret not eating it all.

Hunger is the most agonizing torture. No greater pain can be imagined. It burns inside you like fire, and eats at your body. It kills you slowly but surely. It hits children the hardest. I remember when I was five, I fasted to please God. It started out nicely in the morning, but come noon, I started to shrivel. Near sunset, I nearly passed out. My father rushed toward me with a glass of water and a handful of dates. "Eat this!" he said. "Don't be a martyr!"

My father was a kind and gentle man, not the kind of father who would kill his son to please his God. In wartime, when food became scarce, he would sit there enduring hunger in secret while watching us eat with a proud, fatherly smile on his face. We ate like ravenous wolves while our old man suffered in silence. He was not a hunger artist who starves himself to entertain people, but a martyr for his children. It took him dying for us to appreciate the power of his sacrificial love.

*

Hunger is no game, and our besiegers know it. It's like a weapon to them—a bloodless, invisible weapon, yet more lethal than arms, for it burns constantly inside you. They would not hesitate to starve us into cannibalism, just to show the world that we are less than human.

I smile at my mother's memory. When things soured between us, and things soured between us fairly often, she would go into mad rages, chasing me through the place and screaming in my wake, and vowing to eat a piece of me and drink my blood! I picture her standing there in desperation, biting her lips in suppressed fury, threatening to unleash her demons on me. Her curses were like unripe grapes, sour in the mouth, sweet at heart. She cursed and blessed me in one breath, and asked God to take and save my soul. She cursed the day

I was born and the ground I walked on, but she always kept me in her prayers, which left God bewildered. I forgive her. People always say things we don't mean and rarely give heed to words, for we know they are mere words and not from the heart. Deep inside, I knew my mother would offer me a piece of her to keep me alive.

*

Stranded under a sea of starving children screaming in pain, I smile at the memory of my childhood sweetheart. I remember two little souls chasing the cotton candy cart, barefoot in the dust, looking utterly and purely happy, standing with enchanted amazement and speechless awe while the whirlwind machine spun its magical yarn.

I remember my childhood pals, roving about the camps, roaming the beaten roads without aim, playing soldiers and rebels, chasing the mosquito truck at night while wearing our war masks. Those were happier times, heedless and free, spent in sheer loafing, upended only by war.

My nostalgic reverie is cut short by the sound of children vomiting their food in the vicinity. Wartime food is not for the fainthearted. The bread smells of damp, tastes of dust, and is drenched with our blood.

I miss my mother's food, and now I'm starving. She cooked not for the love of it, but to feed her insatiable children. She cooked out of necessity, but not without imagination, and made good, palatable food, though never enough. There was something quintessentially *motherly* about her cooking. It was rich, authentic, and gratifying. It was to die for. She cooked intensely and with fire. She cooked in old native pots she'd inherited from her mother. Her specialty was lentils with bread, the poor people's meat. It was a large dish, made for a crowd, imbued with love, and enriched with the juice of homegrown lemons that would melt your heart. I did not appreciate that dish then, but I do now.

For dessert? Carob pudding, of course. This ancient native evergreen shrub works magic on the kids, especially when you swirl a little goat milk into the mix. It was heaven in a bowl. If only we knew it!

*

We could live by bread alone, if it existed. People are starving nearby. You can hear their bellies growl. I miss bread. My mother baked it fairly often. It was so delicious it could be eaten alone.

I'm starving down here, perishing into the earth. Give me a piece of hot bread, dipped in native olive oil the color of emerald! I wouldn't mind a dash of honey for my troubles; it pairs well with olive oil on bread.

The olive tree is our national symbol, though it has become sadly endangered, like the people who grow it. To extend its buffer zone along the border, the enemy has burned the olive orchards down to the last tree. You can hear the ashes billow into the darkened sky. Whole acres of native beauty have vanished into thin air. It's a sad sight, watching our olive groves, the seeds planted by our ancestors, burn to ashes.

We take pride in our olive oil, the wine of the dispossessed. We luxuriate in dipping fresh bread in native oil. It's our national dessert, especially during the olive season, at the mill, when the oil comes out, hot and green. My favorite dessert was olive oil and sugar spread on flatbread. Some add honey, which is a luxury. Or jam, which they smuggle through the tunnels, because it's banned here. I hear some have managed to smuggle in chocolate. It must be a rumor, for chocolate is strictly banned in the Strip, because it fills the men with dangerous energy, a dark energy. Or so our besiegers believe.

My poor father believed chocolate was a luxury. Was he in league with our besiegers? He said dates were sweeter, so whenever I craved chocolate, I dug into some dates. When those became scarce, I'd suck on sugarcane, which abounded here once.

A sudden unslakable thirst comes over me, and I pass out, roaming dreamlike in a desert of deprivations —my life under siege.

I smile in my agony as a boy stands over the rubble, picking his nose and licking it, picking and licking. He does it with persistence and desperate intensity that would melt the heart of a stone. I feel sorry for the poor soul; no child can survive on that stuff.

The sad rattle of empty bowls and pots has become the soundtrack of this land. You feel like you are living in an unending nightmare full of sound and fury. I make out a girl, a starving little girl. With an empty bowl in her hand and hunger in her voice, she approaches a stranger, who nods with a hopeless gesture, a hint of an ironic smile, and offers to walk her to a nearby shelter, where she won't be starving alone. Little knowing that hunger is a lonely torment, for it eats silently inside you. It devours you slowly but surely.

*

A strange noise stirs me awake. Straining my ears, I make out a woman, a mother to be exact, stirring rocks in an empty pot to lull her hungry children to sleep. Like a toothless witch stirring her magic brew in a cauldron, hurrying her children into death while praying for their survival. Gone are her teeth, yet still she stirs and clamors.

The image puts a sad smile on my battered face.

I'm not new to hunger, let me tell you. Our land has known more war than peace. So people revel in whatever calm their destiny affords them. They bake their bread with old millstones and stone ovens. There are days when we live on bread alone, when there *is* bread. Bread is our daily fare. And lentils, of course, which perhaps explains why our faces tend to yellow with age. Mother cooked them regularly. She always pleaded with me to eat. "For heaven's sake, son, you look like a skeleton!" That woman was devoted to my belly; my survival was her cross to bear. She stuffed morsels of food into my mouth, and when food was scarce, she fed me morality tales on the virtues of contentment. My favorite features a poor woman who stirs fish bones in her soup pot to coax her starving children to sleep—a fitting bedtime story, especially when hunger steals into your sleep.

I wouldn't mind a bowlful of sardines for my troubles. But fish is rare here, because the fishermen are forbidden to fish free and far. Many spend a whole day in the sea and return empty-handed. One is more likely to fish out a perfect pair of shoes than a fish. Those who venture far out are often drowned and fed to the fish. No wonder our fish are fatty. We live like pirates of our own sea. Some fishermen have despaired and deserted the dear old sea altogether. You can see the tiny old fishing boats standing moored to the harbor wall, ghostlike, shifting with the surf, echoing only to the winds.

But we endure, because we are proud and dignified people. We never beg. We rough it. We bathe in the sea and shower in the godsent rain. When water becomes rare, we drink seawater. When food becomes scarce, which is fairly often, we eat grass and cook tree leaves. Our children are vegetarians, not out of luxury, but because they are so often reduced to eating grass and leafy greens, which is why their faces tend to look green with time, like little aliens. In wartime, when food runs out, we subsist on a wild plant named mallow, which tastes delicious, when properly cooked. In the last war, when famine loomed and mallow vanished, people survived on wild roots. When those were depleted, they rummaged for food and picked grains out of animal manure, which we called *caviar*. We survived that way.

We always survive, because we are not people of worldly extravagances, though like all people, we do crave the nice things. We eat and drink for strength and survival, not from gluttony. Wouldn't we love three meals a day, with snacks in between? But it's a sin to overindulge. Or so we believe. We are light eaters, out of necessity, not urban luxury. We eat to live, though our food is to die for.

*

Lost in reverie, I find myself at hell's gate. I see waves of starving children, gathered at the grand prison's gates with horrified excitement, poking their thin heads and hands through the bars, holding empty bowls, and casting empty stares beyond the gates, squinting into the sunlight like bewildered prisoners.

You hear cheers of hope, and screams of horror, and you wonder what strange tale is weaving itself on the surface. It appears world powers are air-dropping food for the people, which lands either far out in the sea or right on people's heads. Children look at the sky, wondering whether it's going to drop food or rockets, bread or bombs. Food and bombs dropped in one instant, to both kill and feed, in no particular order.

The food drops have left me more mystified than relieved. It's as if the world in its cynical benevolence is teasing us to death. One can hear the shouts of life and death collide under the indifferent skies.

Have you tried this wartime food? It's not for the faint of heart. It's marginally preferable to hunger. It fills you but hollows out your spirits. Bullets are more tolerable! Most packages contain crackers and nuts meant to break your teeth, if you have any left. Others contain dried meat that's more dead than dry. Or something formerly fish. Or canned fruits beyond their expiration dates, with a colorful rot that renders the original fruit a fathomless mystery. Some promise nothing but gum. The food is clearly not fit for humans, or animals, or subhumans. Surely they don't expect starving kids to subsist on gum alone?

*

A salty taste is clinging to my mouth, seeping into my tired skin. It could be my sweat, or perhaps tears. Perhaps it's the sea breeze. Or merely dust. Whatever its origin, it's adding salt to my unhealing wound. My only consolation is that my body will be preserved until I'm discovered and buried properly.

Salt is sacred here. People use it to preserve meat, for they are too poor to afford refrigerators. It's an ancient practice handed down from the ancestors. In wartime, when the enemy bombs the hospitals to let the wounded bleed to death, people turn refrigerators into morgues, and apply salt to preserve the corpses, which perhaps explains why people would rather salt their meat than refrigerate it.

A foul stink sweeps through the underground, like the sour reek of death. It's smothering me with its hot, simoom-like wind, and for long, torturous moments, I can neither hold my nose nor breathe.

From the panic-stricken murmur, a dystopian picture emerges: To tighten the siege, enemy forces have flooded the tunnels with seawater and poison gas. Many have perished underground, buried alive with their food and goods and donkey carts. Many others are dying aboveground. The tunnels are our secret lifelines, our safety belt. Without the tunnels, we would have long perished under siege. This vast labyrinth of underground underpasses resembling a spiderweb is our last hope for survival, and our besiegers know it! Endless wars and unending sieges have rendered us a nation of hobbits.

As I lie contemplating these thoughts, a powerful stench hits me like a foul wind, and I assume someone has died beside me. I hide my disgust, knowing that's how I will smell when my hour comes. Besides, the stink is now my only hope of being found.

*

People gather amid the ruins to pray, and I linger there listening to them with awed admiration. They pray calmly, at ease, as if savoring a fleeting moment of serenity in a place on the verge of annihilation. Some have bleeding wounds. Others have bleeding hearts and seem to be grieving, for they can be heard weeping faintly through prayers, quietly coping with their loss. They all pray to Heaven, as all earthly pleas have fallen on deaf ears.

You need to understand that we pray to Heaven so much not because we are fanatic or delusional people, but because we have no allies on this earth. Outsiders seem to dread our faith, even when it becomes our last resort in a world bent on our destruction. When death looms and despair sets in, people try to cope. They resort to praying, mainly, for it possesses a mystical power that keeps them going.

I always prayed as a child. I feared God; I truly did. I dreamed of Heaven and all the flowing rivers of milk that awaited me up there if I followed the right path. And yes, I was afraid of Hell. Who isn't? I was told that Hell had such a depth that a stone thrown into it would make a seventy-year journey, and that scared the hell out of me. Little knowing that Hell was awaiting us here, on this earth, burning with a thousand fires. For that's what the Strip has become—an infernal perdition teeming with hapless refugees gasping for air and screaming with dying breaths.

My father, praise be, was a tireless prayer. He had a permanent bump on his forehead, a token of lifetime devotion. He had swollen toes, from constant bending. He prayed in a state of total submission, bowing and kneeling, as if unsure about the best way to please his Creator. He was like God's shadow on the earth. His most precious possessions consisted of a prayer rug, worry beads, and a palm-sized copy of a sacred book, which he kept in his pocket for prayers. He treated the book reverently and leafed through it tenderly, lest he damage its spine. I keep that book in my pocket.

I remember those days as I wait here shivering in the cold without so much as a blanket, taking solace in the warmth of my own blood, while coping with a sudden, irresistible desire to pray.

*

I had a dream last night. I dreamed that I was spirited away by my alien friends, or perhaps by ancestral spirits, and taken on a fantastical journey to our bombed house, where I ventured out to try to recover my mother's copy of *War and Peace*. I remembered there was an amulet tucked into it, a good luck charm, which I wished to keep. I also longed to leaf through the book, if only to feel her touch on the pages. When loss runs so rampant, even the slightest residue of lost times becomes a treasure. I'm speaking of my mother's page marks. Those folds, gently creased at the corners, still bear her tender fingerprints.

That woman loved to read, when she could afford it. She read the way my father prayed: deeply and in total submersion. She read not for fun, but to empower herself, to avenge her alienation under siege. She wolfed down foreign romances in translation as if they were native sweets, or bittersweet odes to the beautiful life she never had. Was she, too, dreaming of escape in the silence of her fantasy?

I inherited her love for words. I was a child crazy about words. If only I had known what to do with them! What good are words to a nation under rubble whose screams are nothing but hollow, muted echoes? You may scream your lungs out, but the walls won't budge an inch.

Still, we revere words. We live and die for the glory of words. Sacred or profane, revelatory or mundane, we revel in the splendor of our words. Poetry is our national opium. You meet people in the rubble, bleeding, dying, yet eagerly scribing in blood their last words on the walls in the vain hope of being remembered. All we have left are words, our silent weapons that seem to frighten outsiders, who would rather bomb us into silence than hear any of it. Words are our last bulwark; what defense have we but words? All the tragic things that have happened to us are because we lacked the sense to keep silent.

And besides the amulet I wanted to find in the dream, there would be a family album tucked among the books, a personal history of war and peace. One photo featured three generations of us, none of whom has survived. It was taken by my late uncle, the photographer, in more peaceful times. Another featured father and son marching to stop the war. Innocent times. A third, stashed beside the amulet, belonged to my sweetheart.

I found the place in ruins. There was no *War and Peace*, only war. And not a single photo. The place was defiled and defaced, and every trace of memory erased. Even the sea was blackened with our ink.

I awoke in a cold sweat. I looked around and saw no aliens but myself, a hapless thing buried in the ruins of his home in a dead, dark corner of this cold planet.

Perhaps one should not be too hasty to recover lost times. Sometimes you must accept your doom and embrace your loss.

*

I'm still under rubble, displaced underground, waiting without hope for those willing hands to reach out to me. To judge from the unending murmur, mine is not the worst of displacements. At least you know you've reached the end of your displacement. I hear of people who have been displaced ten times, and are still roaming.

I can hear the sound of great exodus. The ghosted homes, echoing with the silence. The deserted doors, swinging on their hinges. The empty windows, rattling in the wind. The millstones, left running.

I hear the trepidations of exile. People trample over your grave, tumble a bit, rise up, dust themselves off, and resume the journey.

There is a great confusion in the camp. A sea of people, dazed and bewildered, thunder aimlessly in all directions, like windblown waves stirred to frenzy. People step on each other as they make a hopeless dash for the exits, which do not exist. Many risk stampeding as they scramble for the nonexistent safety. They resemble mad waves dashing forward, only to be halted by the breakwaters. It's as if the Tower of Babel has fallen and the people have nowhere to disperse.

Families are in utter panic, carrying mattresses and clothes, food and water jars. People bake their bread in haste, and pack it before it's leavened. Donkey carts are hastily loaded with children and belongings, and bundles that reach the sky. They hit the beaten road on foot and hoof, with wheels and wheelbarrows—the sound of a thousand exiles. All are headed for the gates that are not there!

People sound exhausted, pained and wounded, darting ghostlike from one point to another, lost in the tumult and confusion of the hour, too busy to fathom the tragedy befalling them. Children, newly orphaned, are rambling the streets without aim, following the crowds with no inkling of the destination to which they are headed, like little mice dashing nimbly forward whenever the sun shines on them.

I make out an old woman, pleading to be left to die on her native soil. Perhaps she finds the journey too taxing to complete on foot. Leaning on her son, she winds her way along the beaten road, past my grave, not too slow, but not too fast. She's in no rush to be displaced.

I can hear it all, like the invisible demons of the deep. I can see the heart of darkness casting its deep shadow in my hole in the earth, where nothing but the faint glint of death shimmers.

*

I have never known a destruction so total. I can't see it with my eyes, what a blessing, for I remain buried underground and my eyes are clouded with dust. But I can feel it with my batlike senses, which are sharper in the dark, especially when I space out.

An eerie noise stirs me awake. I cock my ear toward the unfamiliar sound, but I can't make it out. Slowly, a dark, futuristic vision starts to form. It appears our enemy has deployed war robots to kill us, as one can clearly deduce from the way these monsters charge across the surface. They seem determined to kill us all, to the last soul, for only then they can be sure, absolutely sure, that the sun will not rise on this place again.

A sudden distant noise shakes me out of my rumination, like violent thunder on a midsummer day. I hear the heavy treads of tank convoys on the main road, shaking the ground with their mighty thuds, like the sound of a thousand elephants. I assume the Beach Road, once the pride of the coast, is no more. I picture a long stretch of dirt, dark and gray, now scarring the place where the road once passed. The road that mapped the happy venues of my youth no longer exists. It's been erased, defaced, like a paradise reduced to a wasteland.

I picture a landscape, lying scorched and blackened, grayed with the dust of war, like the leftovers of a bad dream. I picture the sky, sad and bereft of color, and the sea, melancholy gray, its lonely shores abandoned by the people. The enemy has always craved our sea, and now that it's become our graveyard, they crave it even more. The beachfront camps will be rendered seaside resorts for the soldiers, who will proceed, without global backlash, to build thriving towns and shiny towers on our bones and ruins. It's always been that way. You can hear the drunken soldiers, parading the streets in a state of murderous euphoria, and how good bad music sounds when they march on top of the ruins of the displaced. They will be enshrined in history books as heroes, and the victims will die nameless. It's always been that way. Victims' stories often go untold, unhailed, unsung by poets, lost to history. It's the murderers who write history, to beautify their crimes.

*

You hear occasional explosions nearby. At first you suspect bombs are raining down. But then a different tale starts to take form. The landscape, it transpires, is riddled with unexploded arms—thousands of leftover bombs buried deep underground and waiting to detonate. You can feel the monsters lurking dormant underneath, ready to unleash death and terror on the heedless surface. Land mines lie strewn across the terrain, dotted with small explosives that look like toys to the children. Smart bombs resembling food cans are left scattered across the toxic earth, planted by soldiers to kill and maim starving children. Those booby traps dot the streets like deathly snares. The Beach Road is sprinkled with them, live ticking bombs lying conspicuous and sinister on the sand with their yellow markings. Some buried explosives have popped up and jumped to the surface like dolphins, wiping out everything that stands. And those are the only dolphins we know.

I think of the tender bodies lying along the main road, bombed beyond recognition. One is lucky to be blind in this doomed place. Or is he? For blindness only sharpens your morbid imagination!

I picture the roads, empty and melancholic, echoing only for the vultures. You see only ruins, wreckage littered along the roads, the skeletal silhouettes of houses, charred fields, gaping craters, the last human ghosts clinging zombie-like to the defamiliarized landscape. You picture corpse-like people, beaten and wounded, wandering, wondering by what miracle they are still alive. Above them, the sky grows dreary and dismal, dense with dust and dark with smoke, so dark that you wonder, *Was the sun blotted out for good?*

Night falls permanently. A gleam of moonlight leaks briefly through the rubble, leaving a sad reflection. Then it disappears, and total darkness sets in. Hell is not as dark. Nothing breathes, save for tireless planes hovering overhead at the altitude of birds, ready to strike.

I have lived twelve wars, and survived as many, but I have never witnessed anything so dystopian. All this time, I have imagined that dystopias existed in books only. But this one is upon us, and beyond imagination. There can be no fiction after this.

*

I may be blind, but the horror is too vivid not to register in the mind. Your sense of vision is acute, and your hearing is supersonic. Your sense of smell is sharper than a shark's. Every sense is heightened tenfold. And then there is the dreadful chatter of a people on the verge of extinction. One hardly needs his sight among this nation of born storytellers. You must hear the unflagging chatterers, spinning their ghastly yarns in your horrified ears as if solicited. There's no escaping it. Your hands tied up under rubble, you can neither plug your ears nor hold your nose. You *must* witness it all, and weep for the others. But no one will weep for you, or sing your song, for you have no song. You are lucky to have breath left in you in this hellscape.

There's no resisting the chatter. For the strange truth is that I'm starting to find company, a sort of dark solace, in this ghastly chatter. It's as if a demon, a death angel, is maliciously feeding me with tales of horror to torture me in my grave, and I do nothing to stop him.

*

Death is rife in the camps, marching on with unhinged fury. Somehow the proximity of it makes me feel more alive than dead. These are moments of sheer horror, save for the secret joy that comes from suddenly realizing what it means to be alive. There is a certain guilty pleasure in being alive while many others have perished, a strange feeling of triumph, deep and shameful, but inescapable.

Yet I haven't the faintest idea what I'm living for, or have survived for. Nothing awaits us out there but ruins, bodies to bury and losses to mourn, and whole lives to rebuild amid the wreck. We have no fight left in us, and no power to rebuild.

There is no hope to go on living when life itself has ceased to exist. Life means nothing to me, and death scares me no more. I'm living only because destiny is blind and acts in strange ways.

*

The renewed bombing has taken me by surprise, for I was under the happy illusion that there was nothing left to bomb. Death is ubiquitous, too common and mundane to make an impression. Its musty reek pervades my body. You wait there wondering how you will die: bomb, rocket, fire, or starvation. Or perhaps grief. Or fright. Or fatigue—there is no shortage of survivors who have perished from exhaustion, consumed by the unending frenzy of escaping death.

Blood is everywhere. You can smell it. It's screaming out of the earth. Wounded people lie on the ground nearby, racked with pain—people with gruesome injuries writhing in great agony, pleading for a lethal injection. But there is no injection, because medicine has been long depleted and hospitals bombed out of existence. Doctors now operate on children without anesthetics, deploying primitive saws made from razor wire. One doctor had to amputate the leg of his own son; he then burst into hysterical tears and collapsed to the ground. There is enough pain in this place to keep Hell glowing. You can hear the doctors pleading with people to weep less and breathe more.

You hear a father, weeping over the body of his headless baby. It's not a pleasant sight to picture. But it's unfolding as we speak, the horror tale unrolling itself. It happens so often that the smartest bombs cause the most primitive and savage deaths. The worst barbarians in human history would be baffled by the grotesque images these bombs have created. The evil wrought here would humble the devil himself. I can picture him, rolling with amusement in his fires.

The smell of death is horrendous. The more time passes, the more horrendous the smell. The whole place resembles a slaughterhouse. Human limbs and body parts are discarded and left to fester and rot. The fortunate ones have lucked out and died. They are in Heaven now. Or so we believe, because we'd go insane if we believed otherwise. And supposing this Heaven exists, it's still a mirage, unreachable to the living dead, the hobbits hereunder, stranded under rubble and all.

*

The bleeding ground of this necropolis is not done speaking, even as the unfolding calamity now threatens to morph into a boring horror story. From the murmur of the rescuers above, an image presents itself. Nameless bodies are spread out all over, rotting into the ground, being eaten by animals. Vultures are hovering over the corpses with festive eyes. Bodies, dismembered, featureless, disfigured beyond recognition, dot the red grounds like pieces of a jigsaw puzzle. You picture a leg here, a hand there, body bits everywhere. You ought to zigzag your way among them as if walking through a minefield. The rest resembles minced meat, for you can smell it, and hear it cry out from the ground.

"Have you seen my son's head?" a frantic father is asking the rescuers. "He has brown eyes and black hair." Some clues!

Children are writing their names on their hands and legs, so that when their little bodies are blown to bits, their remains can be identified. Women are wearing name bracelets, lest they end up buried in mass graves with strangers. Chastity matters, even in death. Men in death throes jot their farewells on the walls with their own blood, as if asking us to remember them and tell their stories. It's human. People wish to be remembered. They want to die with dignity. They want their graves to have names and dates. They want a last address, a visiting place, a landmark, somewhere that survivors can visit and lament their absence. It's human, all too human.

*

Another horror tale starts to come together as I tilt my ears to the eerie canter echoing from the main road. I hear a horse trotting away, slowly, beating the sandy road with heavy hoofbeats. I gather it's a horse-drawn wagon, carrying the dead across the barren wastes.

I fall into a daydream, sailing into those uncertain spaces between life and death. On the main road, a man is riding his horse with the body of a dead child slung over the saddle in front. He's holding the little corpse in one hand, and the bridle in the other. He seems to be riding aimlessly, bound nowhere and everywhere. Perhaps he's looking for a safe spot to bury the body, a place with a surviving landmark he could remember and visit, should he survive.

Maybe being stranded underground is not the worst of destinies. At least I still have my hopes to draw on when the day turns bleak. Sometimes, when pain overtakes me, I hallucinate Heaven. I fancy myself in a happy place, warm and pleasant. But then the howls nearby grow louder and bomb me out of my visions.

*

I might be sad and empty, but I'm not lonely. The place is heaving with displaced and newly orphaned children who have found home in the rubble, a dark safe haven from the bright flames of death.

A young boy draws near, holding a heavy bundle that seems to weigh him down, and he sits amid the broken slabs to catch his breath. He bursts out weeping. From the red drops seeping out of the bundle, I speculate that it contains the body of his little brother.

I wish I could lend him a comforting hand. But being under rubble and nearly dead, I can barely console myself. You are required not only to raise the spirits of others, but sometimes to sustain your own.

On the main road, I hear a bike pedaling away, beating the tattered ground with its heavy treads. I picture a little boy in the harshness of exile. Newly orphaned, he has bundled his baby brother on the back of his bike, together with their belongings and family's remains, and headed for displacement under heavy rain and bombardment. Or perhaps it's a little girl with a ponytail pedaling for her life, carrying a bundle filled with the life she's left behind, or whatever has remained of it.

I can hear the clatter of the bike as it falls.

*

Some moments remain a puzzle to me. I'm speaking of the unrestrained joy that accompanies pulling a whole family from the rubble, which is akin to pulling a victory from the jaws of defeat.

Cheers burst out as a family of forty, having spent twelve days of relentless bombardment hiding in a basement, emerge at last, half alive, half dead. It appears the dead half have perished from starvation. But the other half are breathing still, and that's triumph enough.

Half dead, half alive! I know what that means. I feel that way myself, split into two destinies, of which neither seems to prevail. Sometimes I feel more dead than alive; at others, a lucky mortal in a sea of death.

*

My face beams with a smile as three children sit unperturbed over my grave, wolfing down a donated meal, munching like famished cubs, heedless of the starving being underneath.

I think of my sweetheart. I promised to marry her. Mere words, not from the heart! I shall never start a family. The prospect terrifies me, having a family in this human jungle. Perhaps it's the unending war. Or maybe the fear of losing someone I love. There's only one thing I fear more than my own death, and that's the death of a loved one, perhaps because I no longer have any spiritual strength to draw on. I'm helpless, utterly powerless in the face of loss. People endowed with strength of spirit arouse my envy. Who said my father was powerless? Who said he was a helpless old man? Death is a pill that no one can bear to swallow without something sweet; hence faith, God, salvation, the afterlife. My old man had all these things. He was death's worst nightmare. My father is immortal, made in God's image. Nothing inspires wisdom like death, and my father was lucky to witness many.

With sad admiration, I listen to the children as they devour their meals to the last morsel, sounding happy and grateful. The image of content children in this Golgotha assuages the fires within.

*

I'm lost in a haze. I'm too tired to think, and too distressed to stop thinking. No one thinks on an empty stomach—trust me. You need full guts to rip open your wounds. I'm feeling weak and disoriented. I've clearly lost my bearings. I can no longer reflect on or ponder things. I reminisce mainly to remind myself to stay alive. It hardly matters if you live or die in this inferno, but you follow your survival instinct anyway. I haven't a clue what I'm living for anymore; I'm blanking on it. I remember having dreams, but I can no longer make them out. I remember a certain dream of traveling the world, but seeing how the world has treated us, I have lost my desire to see it.

To my good luck, a bomb drops nearby, and I lurch violently and lose my senses, and almost instantly sail into another of my reveries.

*

It's astonishing how much human drama one can weave from just sounds and voices. One feels as if spinning an unending spool of yarn. So much loss, too many deaths, but they are never quite the same.

I'm not new to death. I witnessed many funerals as a child. My most vivid memories are of funerals of fallen martyrs. They were my daily rite, my pastime. I saw a good many dead faces: colorless, featureless, sad, gone, some smiling still. I knew for whom the bell tolled, and I learned by heart what the heartless headstones said: the names and dates and hours, the lives that had suddenly frozen in time. I heard the elegies, the howls, the lamentations, the ululations. I remember it all in awful detail. The sealed eyes, the faint odor rising from the earth, the fragrance of native incense, and the perfumed bodies of martyrs. The loud cries of mourning, which could be heard far and wide. I remember the weddings that awaited martyrs in Heaven, the bathed bodies, the white shrouds, the green coffins. The earthbound faces. They say that earthly people, who take on the color of earth, can hardly be distinguished from the soil when laid in the ground.

But these deaths now are nothing like any I have seen. Bodies are hurled into gaping holes, and stashed underground with a heap of sand, without so much as a bath. No death more undignified can be imagined. No farewell, no ceremony. No fuss or hoopla.

There are no white shrouds left. People are buried with their clothes. You hear a father, weeping, pleading with the gravediggers to leave him the clothes of his dead son before he's buried. People struggle to keep whatever souvenirs or reminders of their loved ones they can, whatever last mementos they can save. You hear a mother in the clutches of madness, clinging to the dress of her slain child, red with blood. She puts up a good fight, to judge from the howls, but then she breaks down and lets go of it, for there is no shroud left for the child.

No coffins left. When I was a child, our camp had a green wooden coffin, which the dead had to share. It was nailed together before the war and served the departed a good while, when life was precious and death rare. I never imagined that a coffin would one day be a godsend.

*

Life is a strange thing. One moment, you are a human being with grand dreams and hopes. The next, you're buried in an ever-shrinking pit with no hope of rescue, an unbending hollow wide enough to suck you in, but narrow enough to become your grave. My only wish, now that I'm both feet in the grave, stranded without hope in this morbid hole, dead to the outside world, is to be discovered and buried properly, in the fashion of my ancestors. Let that be my last wish.

I have lost my bearings. I feel like I'm living in a timeless purgatory, a dreadful nonplace. When night falls, the bombing jets become my only source of light. In the day, the clouds of destruction blanket the sky. There are times when the Strip plunges into utter darkness, and there's no telling day from night. The clouds of war block the sun, and the moon, and the very air we breathe. It's a blessing in disguise. Darkness shelters us from the horrors of the day, throwing one veil over us all. Light only exposes us to hostile drones and hastens our death. The enemy likes to strike lit houses because they know people must be living there. I smile at the memory of my father screaming his eternal wartime cry: *Lights out! Lights out!*

*

I'm still underground, buried alive, sweating like a naked seal. The relentless bombing has created a blast wave that travels in all directions. Night falls, and for a brief hiatus, nothing stirs—not a leaf or a wisp of air. You look around and see a barren ghostland, a broken land where night gives no shelter from the heat, and the day no relief. Heat rises from the ground as from a fire, full of stirring devils. I picture the rescuers, gathered at Hell's gate, bathing in their own sweat, wiping their faces with their sleeves. Even the sky is dirty. Flares whizz past. Fighter jets cruise overhead at low altitude, ready to strike anew. You feel worn out and utterly depleted, your feet hardened, your face dust-beaten, your head bloated, your eyes needled with dust and ashes, your body doused in sweat. You lie there nearly breathless, panting like a flogged dog, glistening like a hairless cat, the smell of hot blood clinging to your nose. If you are alive, it's only because the angel of death is busy reaping lives elsewhere.

*

Last night was horror incarnate. I believe it was nighttime, yes, because a hint of full moon was still visible from my grave.

A cosmic force hit the main hospital nearby, and rendered it a pile of rubble. The blast was so colossal that fragments burned their way into my hole. By what miracle I survived, it's hard to tell.

The hospital is no more. Women are now giving birth in pools of blood. You hear a woman in the pangs of childbirth. She lets out heavy breaths, agonizing cries of pain, followed by the familiar cries of a newborn—a new life born in the rubble.

People speak of horrors I never knew existed. It's like magical realism that's more magical than real. You hear of pregnant women undergoing cesarean sections without anesthetics, dying while giving birth—dying to give life, like the tragic martyrs of yore. Babies in incubators evacuated, many perishing on the way. Bereaved fathers, holding armfuls of shrouded children, processing in silence.

Come nighttime, the whole place runs out of power and plunges into total darkness. Newborn babies die in the cradle. The poor souls never saw the light of day. It must be tragic, dying in the cradle while a whole life is waiting for you. Or perhaps it's a mercy in disguise.

I brace for a similar fate. It appears that mounting rubble from the bombed hospital has blocked the last access to my grave and rendered it nearly impossible to discover. And even before that, there was little hope for me. To reach survivors, rescuers have to navigate through mountains of fallen concrete that seems to pile up indefinitely. You can hear them in the vicinity, shouting in their mad staccato, humming in low and suppressed whispers lest they attract the soldiers who seem intent on wiping out the last shred of life here. I can neither shout nor whisper. I have lost my voice. Perhaps I never had one. I have lost my desire to resist. Resistance means a daring and direct look in the eyes, a boiling of the blood, a muted protest in the bones—I have none of that left.

*

Every hour seems to bring a grim new record of death and destruction. One moment you hear people scrambling for survival. The next, they are gone, like windblown grains of dust. These bombardments are as relentless as they are merciless. Even the rain takes a breath!

People are praying for rain, to pacify the fires of war, but mainly to wash away the blood. But even our rain, once pristine and heavenly, comes down dark and ashen. It rains death and destruction, pours from our joyless skies like the dark tears of the gods. Our clouds are nothing but the smoke of war parading in the sky.

When the first hints of clouds loomed across the desolate sky, I kept my mouth wide open, hoping the rain would find its way to it. And when, this morning, the first rains of autumn briefly poured down at last, the children forgot all about their agonies and played in the godsent rain, and I sensed in their cries of joy a glimmer of their former happiness, a kind of joy never registered in the history of emotions. It was a lovely spectacle, while it lasted. Soon enough, the clouds grew dark as the jets started bombing the rain and showering us with death. And when the kids, in a spark of native defiance, took to the nearby beach to assert their right to happiness, the enemy bombed the beach, and the waves, and those who braved them. And when our defiant children grew tired of the bombing and gathered on top of the ruins to fly their kites—it's a miracle that any of them survived. What good are kites in a place domed with ashen skies?

A faint smile lands on my face as I remember my sweetheart—the sweet memory of us, flying our kites in better and kinder days, dreaming of love and romance, and the freedom we never had.

*

Sometimes, when I daydream, I imagine myself in possession of great supernatural powers, fighting mighty tanks with my bare chest and primitive homemade weapons. Masked like Batman, armed with a slingshot and stones, I fire on enemy tanks at close range. I trap soldiers, and liquidate them with homemade dynamite. In my unbridled bravery, my flight of fancy, I have morphed into a Samsonian martyr, bringing down houses on the heads of my besiegers, who have converted our homes into military bases. Having turned our ruins into trenches, I ambush soldiers inside abandoned houses and tear them down on their heads. I batter tanks and bulldozers with rocket-propelled grenades, and gun down trigger-happy soldiers as they bask in their fleeting victories.

I'm a righteous god bringing justice to the oppressed. I *am* justice! You must've seen me, sniping that soldier with chilling precision! There I sit, perched in my position, quiet and birdlike, hiding in the rubble of our bombed home, biding my time, eyeing the monster with my cool yet deadly patience, hunting him down while crying with disbelief—the disbelief of a powerless man who finds himself suddenly empowered. Revenge is a noble feeling indeed. It's justice.

*

From the dark cocoon of my underground grave, I can see the terrible aspects of death and destruction rumbling on the ravaged surface, unfolding in vivid detail, unveiling one horror after another, layer after layer, like a shriveled artichoke. I have lost my eyesight, but I still have my vision, which seems to darken with every moment.

People speak of a truce. *Truce*—the word is music to my ears! I survive by the mere promise of it. But then, what good are truces? While a truce might stop the bloodshed and offer a fleeting relief, it will only enhance the agony. A truce will give bereaved parents and orphaned children time to bury and mourn their loved ones, and fathom the depth of their loss. It will bring us face to face with the destruction wrought upon us, and the abyss the incessant bombing has left in its wake. War keeps us distracted. When under constant bombardment, you are busy surviving and saving others, fighting for your life, or perhaps hoping to die and reunite with your loved ones above. You have no time on your hands to reflect on your loss, or weep for your dead, or comprehend the scale of your grief, or contemplate the apocalyptic destruction of everything you knew and loved, for even under siege, you still find things to love. You are too deaf and blind from the rattle of war to notice the calamity unfolding about you. You keep reeling from one calamity to another, without the time to grasp any. A truce will lay bare your loss and the destruction that's presently clouded in the fog of war. Now, you're madly looking for your next safe haven. But come the truce, you will be looking into the abyss.

*

I have taken to praying of late. Prayer sets me free. For one feels as if in a prison here, hemmed in behind walls, cooped up in a grave that grows more inescapable every hour. Here I sit, stranded under piles of rubble, dying slowly, feeling like a captive abandoned by his captors.

Unable to move freely in my condition, I pray in my mind, with a slight movement of the eyes. That's how my wounded mother prayed. I'm coming to the conclusion that faithlessness is a peacetime luxury. No one can humanely survive this evil and emerge sane without faith to draw upon—the spiritual power and the inner strength to shove evil away. It gives me solace, and helps me cope. I'm not sure whether Heaven exists, but there must be one, if only to console the innocent who died in vain. One can say the same about Hell, a place filled with warmongers and baby killers. Or so one hopes.

And yet this war has redefined Hell and Heaven for me. When I close my eyes and pray, I dream not of the Heaven above, but the one we have lost here. So I pray with nostalgic melancholy.

*

Sometimes, when the murmur becomes too dreadful to bear, I want to scream at the people to tone it down—to tell them that your tales, O miserable creatures of God, have made deafness a sweet prospect! I *pray* for a crack of thunder to quell their voices into merciful silence, a great flood where all these sounds may vanish under a smothering layer of foam!

And as if by miracle, the murmur suddenly vanishes, eerily vanishes. I assume it's the temporary vacuum that follows a massive bombing. Nothing bespeaks destruction like the eerie silence that follows. But it's better thus. I can relish the quiet, while it lasts.

From the perspective of the moon, this sad place likely resembles a red spot, without the warmth, as if reeling from a biblical disaster, or an earthquake, or a nuclear catastrophe. From the perspective of extraterrestrials gazing down on us, this might look like the end of civilization, the end of times, hastened by benevolent ones who believe they must step over dead bodies to create civilization anew.

I feel lonely, without a people, alone and forsaken in the dark, cold solitude of my grave, where nothing stirs but the interminable tidings of loss and death, and the frightful silences in between.

But then the horrified chatter overhead resumes with renewed vigor and verve, and I breathe with relief.

*

You may wonder, and rightly so, how I get wind of these tales while being hopelessly stranded under rubble? I'm not sure. I have been wondering about it myself. I might be dead, and my soul hovering over the dead homeland. Or perhaps I'm hallucinating, fading into a mirage of my parched imagination. Perhaps I'm a ghost, have always been, born under siege and all. Or maybe I have been abducted by aliens and endowed with the godlike power of seeing it all. Perhaps I'm nothing but a zombie, one of the living dead, but aren't we all? How often have I heard the children scream out, "Zombie! Zombie!" and I immediately knew that some lucky wretched soul had emerged from the rubble at last? But we are not zombies, though the sweat we exude under the earth makes us look bad. We smell of dry blood only because we fled our bombed homes before we had a chance to shower. If we look sick, it's because this war has brought us more diseases than we knew existed. They are ravaging us, killing us faster than bombs.

Buried underground with no hope of escape, I seem to have developed a new sense. For all the darkness underneath, I can envision things vividly. My mind is astute, my heart receptive. My imagination sharpened, it renders sounds into images with the speed of light. It's a curse, a truly torturing curse, this human imagination!

*

I think I'm dying, growing breathless with hunger, and the fires within. Imagine dying from hunger in the land of milk and honey!

Children roam the rubble rummaging for food, and the more they roam, the farther away moves the mirage. They say they miss eggs, though they have only a faint memory of what eggs look or taste like. Here is a hint: They're oval; white on the outside, yellow on the inside.

It's amazing what an egg can do to a child these days. It's happiness incarnate. The rubble teems with them, children of Heaven, the dreamless little souls to whom eggs are manna. I can see it all, for while hunger ravages your body, it gives wings to your imagination. An orphaned child finds a raw egg for the first time in weeks. Crying with joy, he holds it with trembling hands lest it break, like a surgeon holding a human heart in a glass container. Clinging fast to it with both hands through the ruins, he does not bother to wipe away his happy tears. An egg can be a lifesaver, even when there's little left to live for.

When I think about it, my hole in the earth resembles a cracking egg. I feel like a bird curled in its eggshell, fighting to burst free through the cracks, waiting for a gleam of sunshine to hatch out, but the light does not shine and the bird is losing vigor and waning.

*

There's music in everything, even death.

Joy sneaks in through the ruins. A group of children are dancing to the tune of drones buzzing overhead, surrounded by crumbled homes turned coffins, bombed schools, and endless piles of rubble. Their undefeated spirits defy nature herself. You hear them, sliding down a fallen roof, or climbing a shattered wall, their little faces bright with rare joy, a gleam of bewildering happiness in their eyes.

I might be blind, but I'm not deaf to the misery about my ears. A girl shivers over my grave, trembling violently. You can hear her tender bones rattle together like a skeleton dancing. She must be cold, without so much as a blanket. She's trying to find a doorstep to sit on, a space to keep herself warm. It would do her good. I barely have a shirt on, but the rubble keeps me warm. But for the rubble, I would be long frozen. I remember having a bagful of clothes, in preparation for imminent exile, which I lost in the panic of survival. It's tragic to lose the last bag of your belongings, but compared to the unspeakable horrors I have witnessed here, I would rather lose a bag than find myself in one.

I listen to the poor little child as she pulls out a matchbox, and goes on kindling one match after another with evident frenzy. You hear a nervous scrape, and a hiss, a scrape, and a hiss. Then the music stops.

*

For all the destruction wrought upon this place, some people still refuse to accept their doom. A man, with his boy at his side, is rebuilding his bombed house from the ruins. He seems in a special hurry, speaking rapidly and in staccato bursts, as if keen to enjoy his new abode before it's bombed anew. He promises to pay the boy for his work when the war ends. I would let out a cry for help, but I have long since lost my voice, though I do take solace in their hopeful little chatter. I relish the sound of hammers striking with the vigor of life itself. Endless wars have made us a nation of tireless builders. I remember my father, laboring with his bare hands, pausing only to wipe his sweat, mixing the mortar, laying the bricks, nailing the walls, sending every nail home with a simple blow of his hammer. And there I was, a boy of five, feeding nails into his waiting hand, gazing with awe at his craft, like an ancient sage marveling at the miracle of Creation.

I shiver down to my frame as I entertain the prospect of someone rebuilding his home on top of the rubble with me underneath. It's not far-fetched!

*

It amazes me that for all the relentless anguish, people refuse to declare defeat. Don't you hear those glad ululations filling the desolate skies? The scene is not hard to conjure up. In a rare show of native resilience, a couple get married in a refugee tent nearby. It's defying fate and nature, but life must carry on, especially when human loss is so rampant. Nothing stirs matrimonial desires like war. My parents married in the war, many wars ago. I was conceived in wartime, which is hardly remarkable, for it's always been wartime.

Hope gleams, and as quickly dies out, and glad ululations give way to horrified lamentations when the bombing resumes, and the newlyweds, heedless of the fury of the skies, are killed in their fleeting happiness. I have yet to witness a shorter and bloodier honeymoon.

*

Tragedy has spared no one. And you know it's tragic when you start speaking of your loved ones and everyone you knew in this doomed place in the past tense. Today I received the news I have dreaded for days: My childhood sweetheart is no more. She was killed in a bomb strike, with the rest of her family. I still keep her painting somewhere. The landscape, which no longer exists, remains intact in it, alive in her vision, like an imprint left by a dream. Oh, the happy delusion of art! Perhaps we will meet in Heaven. We could marry then.

*

In the dark solitude of my grave, I weep for my sweetheart. I remember a beautiful girl on the threshold of womanhood, perched birdlike in her seaside window, her hennaed hair wafting freely in the shore breeze, casting her dreamy gaze toward the waiting horizon.

Perhaps there was no horizon, nothing but the usual indignities of life under siege: a land swollen with refugees, and a sea teeming with the displaced, and a sky fraught with dreadful possibilities.

I remember two young dreamers in the thrill of nameless joy, standing on the ancient rock facing the sea, holding hands, gazing away, dreaming of freedom and escape, burning to go. But there was nowhere to go. War was raging, and the sea roaring, yet they stood gazing, hearts beating, lips trembling, ready to discover love and its perils, and experience the first stirrings of desire in a place where nothing stirs but the sound of broken dreams and promises.

Love is a strange force. It creates the illusion of an unbreakable union, a powerful bond stronger than death, and when death does part you, you sit there utterly mystified, staring into the sheer frightful abyss the monster has left in its wake, unable to fathom your loss.

*

The day brings no relief. Exile has spared no one, save for those displaced under rubble. One can hear its winds, howling, blowing in every corner of the earth, land, and sea. There is the initial chaos, the inevitable exodus, the sad spectacle of horrified people fleeing terror to more uncertain terrors. I picture the abandoned houses, echoing in the winds. The wet clothes still hanging on lines in the windows. The meals left uneaten, the water left boiling, the coffee left brewing.

Drifting into my reverie, I see a sea, a roaring sea, filled with the displaced. I see a people in the madness of exile, fleeing to the unknown, filing in a silent procession from which not even a grunt can be heard, marching past their bombed houses with downcast faces and tears in their eyes, vanishing into the waiting darkness, never to return. I can see them all. The mad refugees plagued by hallucinations of return, who keep their tents unfolded like a flag of permanent defeat. The women forsaken by Heaven, who abandon their prayer rugs in the dust. The disenchanted men who fold their mats and proceed without protest. The madman who believes he could divide the sea with a wave of his hand. The panicked mother who jettisons her blanket overboard to unburden the ship, with her newborn still wrapped within. The disheartened men and women who seal their memories in a bottle and cast them into the open sea.

To grasp what it means to be displaced, imagine a strip of sand on an abandoned beach on a midwinter day. Each grain of sand is a nameless speck among countless others, but every grain has its own story and destiny. Yet when the great inexorable storm thunders ashore and sweeps away the sand, what is individual and unique melts into one tragic whole.

Perhaps exile will be kinder to us. There's nothing left for us here, no homes, hopes, or dreams, nothing but an unfamiliarized landscape, reduced to a moonscape, and rendered truly unlivable.

Exile has become a sweet mirage for many. Besieged by land, air, and sea, people have nowhere to go. All escape routes lead to certain death. The earth is a burning hellscape, the skies a low-hanging hell, and the sea a giant tomb waiting to suck us in. They can tunnel as far as they please, but they would eventually resurface along with a cloud of blown-up mine shrapnel. Many have perished that way. There's nothing but death at the end of the tunnel. Our land in flames, burned down to the last home, we feel like we are standing at the edge of the desert.

*

The prospect of staying is more terrifying still. You hear tales, each more horrific than the last, and you lie there trying, in your undeluded mind, to separate fiction from reality. But no matter how hard you try, reality triumphs over fiction and proves more harrowing. Every tale, every sound, is so dreadful that it makes you cherish the safety of your grave.

You hear people bustling close by. A blast follows, and the voices eerily vanish. You wonder what invisible force, what massive power, has muted them so swiftly. Then you hear hysterical laughter echoing from the scene, and realize it belongs to soldiers having fun. For no one laughs here anymore, except the murderers. There they sit, unperturbed, blowing up houses and people with remote controls in their hands, the latest innovation of human evil.

You hear a drone roaming over the camp, making the sound of a crying baby. Then you hear the sound of people dashing out to help the imaginary baby, followed by a deluge of bemused bullets.

There they sit, laughing to themselves, basking in the shade of their crime. Unsatisfied, they proceed to celebrate, dancing on the bones of dead children in a state of murderous ecstasy. You can hear them, walking among the dead, smiling to themselves with gratified complacency, indulgence in their bloodshot eyes. Now and then they will claim a slain girl's necklace as a token of victory. Or sleep mockingly in an empty crib that belonged to a child now dead. Or try on the underwear of a murdered girl for the fun of it. The monsters have dethroned the Prince of Darkness and danced on his grave. No darker victory can be imagined.

*

I'm trembling with rage and fury, my body threatening to collapse, the stench of wet blood clinging to my nose. I resist a constant urge to vomit. My body bursts into scarlet ire, the kind you reserve for your worst enemy. My heart rails and fumes. I feel in the grip of madness, my eyes glowing with crimson fire, blood flooding my face and rushing to my ears, my teeth set on edge, my whole body a volcano threatening to erupt. The native is a ticking bomb indeed! A warlike fever overtakes me, wiping away every last vestige of fear or sadness. It's as if all the torture and humiliation of the past days has boiled over. I pull out my imaginary gun and shoot the monsters right in the face. I've always daydreamed about shooting my tormentors. I imagine whipping out my deadly weapon and yelling out my revenge as I gun the bastards down, without mercy or remorse, laughing hysterical, triumphant laughter. We natives invented the art of silent resistance, remember? Resistance means a daring and direct look in the eyes, a boiling of the blood, a muted protest in the bones. Why should I die quietly when there's still a howl in me?

But no sooner have I launched my silent resistance than I declare defeat. Give up, it's hopeless, futile, laughable! My whole world starts to crumble, and my spirit goes under. I divert my thoughts away from rebellion, imagining in my fancy that the monsters can sense my rage. The devil has four eyes. Or so we believe. The soldier is a raging monster; he acts like a monster, and he expects you to treat him like one. For a moment, I ponder screaming, but I think better of it and cling to my silence. But not for long. For as I sit entertaining these violent thoughts, a flying grenade hits the place and sets it ablaze, and the soldiers disperse, and I find myself clinging again to my dear life.

*

Some terrors are better left to the imagination.

In the ruins of the main hospital, one can hear the undeniable footfalls of soldiers taking ten people inside at a time. Then ten gunshots are heard, then the soldiers come out to bring in a new group.

In a dark, cold corner inside the hospital, a woman, a young girl to be exact—some horrors are better left untold!—a young girl screams to the heavens, her scream the sound of a thousand agonies. I shiver down to the bone. I picture my sweetheart. I take solace in the belief that the victim in question is not my sweetheart. Some solace! She has a tender voice, my sweetheart, but this woman, this wretched girl, has lost her voice. She was *robbed* of her voice. For two agonizing hours, she screams and pleads, pausing only to weep. The rest is silence. There are shots in between, while this horror lasts, likely intended for those who have ventured to rescue the poor girl.

I'm recounting these horrors firsthand and in real time because so often the trauma dulls the memory. Subterraneans are a traumatized race, which is why our recollections are often fragmentary, frantic, and hazy. What makes our stories tragic is not what they purport to tell, but what they *refuse* to tell—all the unspoken horrors and unholy terrors, open wounds left to heal on their own. Perhaps time will intervene in some measure to lend an azure tint to our story. Perhaps one day the poets of the world will compose epics to tell of our saga, though we won't be there to savor the glory.

*

The children of this land are made of steel, and for all the unspeakable loss wrought upon them, they refuse to accept defeat.

I smile in my agony when a child reporter walks amid the ruins of her house, and proceeds with her toy camera to document the massacre that has claimed her family. Red Flour, she calls it. "Have you heard the story of the bread that was murdered before it was leavened?"

Go, little lamb, spin your sad yarns and bring them to my ears!

She puts on a good pretend show. She speaks with a solemn air, and a soothing voice. With shocking calm that defies reality and baffles the old, she sits on a tattered sofa amid the remains of her bombed house, and gives her report about the horrors of war, her vision for peace, and her hopes for a better future. She speaks of *steadfastness*, a word so laden with meaning that it nearly collapses under its own weight. Her native eloquence puts the global silence to shame.

I'm starting to relish her company, this lovable chatterbox. The little one sounds quite fluent in worldly matters. She speaks of freedom and liberation, and all those abstract concepts that have long baffled philosophers. She speaks of human dignity and worth, and invokes, bless her innocent heart, the universal declaration of human rights. Excuse me if I laugh, but buried under rubble for so long, I barely remember what it means to be human.

At last, she reads her will: "Toys to friends. Clothes to cousins, and if no one survives, to charity. Shoes to the poor—after washing them, of course."

*

Night falls, casting a dark veil upon the rubble, and in the cold solitude of my grave, I travel back to kinder times.

Life was not a paradise, but it was a tolerable hell, and we endured it. We lived for the little joys that life under siege afforded us. The Beach Road was beautiful, stretching proudly along the coast, teeming with street vendors and flanked by moorings and small boats. The streets were bustling with life, choked with refugees. The roads were unpaved but well traversed—the sound of four million feet. Some people traveled on donkeys. Those beasts are stubborn, but they never tire or whine.

They preserve and endure, like the people who ride them, and they are more grateful than horses. Horses are a loyal species, if you know how to treat them. My grandfather was a horseman in his day, a born knight. Or so he claimed. They say that when he died, his horse refused to leave his grave. The poor animal stood there in brooding silence, as if mourning his departed knight. Dying from grief shortly after, the horse was buried beside him.

I have the faintest recollection of my grandfather. I remember an old man leaning on his cane, wearing his traditional scarf, fiddling with his worry beads, smiling sometimes. He called me *little ghoul*, perhaps to scare my enemies. Somehow the sweet whiff of his pipe survives in my memory, but his face eludes my recollection. His death, like his life, remains a puzzle to me. He lived many lives and survived many wars. He was a refugee from the past. For many years, the old man sat quietly on his doorstep, smoking his pipe and waiting for death to come and wash the past away. He died quietly in his bed, a shameless, leisurely death, if you ask me. I was five when he died. I went to the cemetery and stood by his grave, waiting for a word, a sign of what had happened to us. There was nothing but dreary silence. His painful past died with him.

The past was his past, and history *his* story.

*

Seven days under rubble—I know because I have heard the Sunday bells ring twice. It's been a week of breathless terror. They say on the seventh day God rested, but these monsters never rest. For seven unending days, they have blown up homes for fun. They would plant a bomb, and with a remote control in hand, detonate it with the people inside. Then cheers were heard among the howls.

For seven wretched days, they have set fire to homes, and burned families alive, women and children rendered piles of ashes. You hear of children burned at the speed of light, blackened by the fire but still miraculously alive, breathing through their pain. It must be a terrifying sight, if you can picture it. They say the raging fire is so vengeful it melts down the bones and marrow along with the skin until you can no longer tell human ashes from mere dust.

You can feel the flames vying for a toehold in the rubble like a sun unhinged. If I wanted to be cremated, I would say it in my will!

It's sad to go this way, reduced to ashes and smoke, taken beyond decay. Who will enrich the soil if our dust is scattered in the river? How can one be resurrected that way? How can he ascend to Heaven? Bury me, unite me with the soil, feed me to the worms. Bury me after the fashion of my ancestors in a spotless white shroud, a casket of unvarnished pine. Is that too much to ask of destiny?

O fire, beacon of light and torment! I remember when I was a child, and I was a child once, I heard the story of the ancient deity who stole fire from the gods and gave it to humanity. I remember I was in awe of that god—what was his name? But now, having witnessed this horror unfold in real time, I wish that god had been burned with his secret!

To escape the maw of death, many survivors, no wonder, have taken refuge in the rubble, the sanctuary of this subterranean world.

*

I scream in my silent agony as a battalion of rats dashes past me in a mad hurry. I haven't survived the fires to be devoured by rats!

Rats and other rodents have taken over the ruined homes, feasting quietly on the decomposed bodies that remain uncovered, which abound in the rubble. These wild little monsters are lurking everywhere, feeding freely on the dead, and growing fatter from the fare. They seem to be the only living beings that have fattened up here, besides the vultures.

Sometimes, in a spark of wishful inventiveness, I try to embellish what's unfolding here and inject it with a dose of dramatic flair. But whenever I embark on these dramatizations, the reality turns uglier than the worst flights of my imagination. It seems that while native imagination has its limits, human cruelty is boundless. The atrocities I have witnessed here defy all horror fiction and humble the darkest dystopias. Writers will look upon this place with unforgiving despair. There's no fiction after this, and no poetry.

*

I'm tired to death. I'm sick with sadness and despair, and there's no healing me. There is no hope for me, and there never was any.

Death has never been more imminent. But I'm not afraid. I have witnessed too much death from my grave to fret about my own mortality. My only regret is that I did not die in the first instant of bombing, blown away in my sleepless dreams. A precise bomb could be a blessing, when you think about it. It would've spared me the dreadful torture that's often reserved for survivors, the maddening prospect of awaiting death, wishing it, confounding it with life.

Sometimes I fantasize about martyrdom—to thrust myself into hostile fires and end my suffering. But martyrdom will not end my suffering. It will only please my enemy, and I would be twice as tortured knowing that my tormentors were gloating at my martyr's death. I shall cling to my right to survive, for it's the only right that's left me. I should resist death, yes, for that's the only resistance left. It would be a shame to sleepwalk into the abyss without so much as a fight. If I burn myself alive in a fit of symbolic martyrdom, no one would probably notice, for the whole Strip is engulfed in fire, and the world is too blind to see it or celebrate my honorable death.

Sometimes I fancy myself dying a Samsonian death, wearing a suicide belt and taking a soldier or two with me. But I'm too spineless for that, too gutless. I wouldn't have the heart to pull the trigger. It's laughable anyway—where am I supposed to find a suicide belt in this nonplace? I'm not the martyr kind. I've never held a gun, hardly a slingshot. I was fated to fight with my pen. Oh, father!

The faint cries of a child stir me and cut short my reverie. I picture a sad little boy, a newly orphaned child, standing alone amid the rubble, unable to grasp the depth of his loss, and I remember that, like him, I have nothing left to lose. The Strip was my family, and now it's gone. The Beach Camp was my home, and it's no more, gone in smoke and ashes, reduced to mountains of rubble. Those slain children were the children I never had, and will never have, now that I'm virtually dead. Every trace of human connection I had in this place was erased, obliterated, like it never existed. All the loved ones and loved things are gone, and what's gone, we say, stays gone.

*

Miracles still happen in this doomed place, but never quite perfectly. Remember the newborn who was saved by a miracle from the womb of her dying mother, becoming the sole survivor of her family? She died this morning. Orphaned upon arrival, she was born and died nameless.

I think of my mother. She must be in Heaven right now, whether or not Heaven exists. She suffered much in this world, and whatever destiny awaited her in the next, she's in a better place.

I think of my sweetheart—what has become of her? It's a tad vain, to hope for the survival of your loved ones when so many have perished.

I think of my people, my poor, humble people who never knew peace in this land, who pray to Heaven and expect nothing of this earth, who go under when the earth trembles and come out when the sky falls. Who bury their dead without ceremony and go about their lives.

I think of my homeland, my ravaged homeland that no longer exists, or perhaps exists only as a vestige of its former glory. I love this land. I love it from the river to the sea. I love its mountains, and valleys, and the soil that's drenched with the blood of my ancestors.

*

Sometimes, in the delirium of despair, I see all the slain children rising from the dead and ascending to Heaven in a grand state of collective resurrection, their heads white with dust, the dry blood still clinging to their faces. I see the little souls who died in the cradle put on angelic wings and fly over the liberated homeland. I see the orphaned children reunite with their parents, and head together to the grand liberation ceremony. I see the young lovers who were murdered in the spring of their happiness, basking in the keen native sun, tasting freedom for the first time. I see all the displaced ones, marching back home, holding their keys of return, kneeling down and kissing the soil.

I see my family gathered in the old beach house, my sister crawling on the marbled floor, myself swinging in the old hammock, dreaming my dreams, my brothers basking happily in the shade of our pomegranate tree, my parents watching us avidly with admiration.

At long last, I see my sweetheart, waiting on the old seaside rock like a beautiful mermaid, her native hennaed hair flowing in the wind, the waves roaring gently under her feet, her anklets tinkling softly in the breeze, smiling without an inkling of her tragic death. There she sits, admiring the sea, worth all the silver it resembles, where all those who drowned in the manic panic of exile are being carried ashore by the caring waves, safe and sound, and marvelously alive.

The strangest thing then happens. The dead, taking pity on the living, and defying the laws of nature, stage the most unforeseen rebellion in human history. They start rising from the graves and the ashes, and chasing enemy soldiers through the streets. Nothing terrifies our oppressors like the sight of dead natives marching. With the spirits in hot pursuit, the soldiers cast their arms into the road and fall to the ground. But the spirits continue to march, homebound, as if carried by the winds of return. Perhaps there's truth in the old belief that when a good refugee dies, he returns home. I never imagined that death could be a cherished prospect. Perhaps we should all start out dead.

There is a powerful truth in the old belief that the soul travels after we die. If there is no Heaven, we must invent one, if only for the sake of the children who were murdered in the cradle. It would be inhumane to believe otherwise.

*

I feel like a dead man condemned to perish in prison, except that my cell is made of rubble. A prisoner would likely cope with his fate by dreaming of his freedom, or conjuring up a loving memory. But a man under rubble has no such refuge, because he knows that outside the shattered landscape, neither freedom nor love exists. He's lucky to be buried deep and spared the unfolding horror above his head. He would be fortunate, privileged, *blessed* to be dead—a chosen one.

Perhaps I was destined to live and tell the tale. When my grave is discovered and I'm rescued, I will pen down these horrors on paper for all the world to read. I will put those monsters in my book, and it won't be flattering! I always wanted to write. Our family fable has it that I emerged from my mother's womb with my fingers in a tripod grip, ready to hold a pencil. The Muses spoke to me in the cradle. Or so I believed.

In recounting these events, I have not considered myself as merely relating a series of supernatural terrors. For all the horrors described here, the narrative adheres to the basic principles of humanity, whose lust for blood and destruction has been well preserved and documented throughout history. I must confess, I was always suspicious of those historians of war and the unspeakable horrors they professed to describe, but having witnessed those horrors myself, I now absolve them. The atrocities committed here overshadow any I have read about in history books. Historians will scratch their heads over what happened here, and how, on earth, it was allowed to happen. But it happened, and will happen again, for there will always be wars, and more wars, and still other wars. It's human, all too human.

*

Imagine my amazement when I awake from my dreadful nightmare and find myself the last survivor of a people now dead.

It seems the war has ended, but only because life here has ended.

My position is not one to envy. Humanity has yet to invent a word for a people's orphan. *Peopleless* comes to mind, but it hardly does justice to my condition. No one can survive on his own, and even though I have, I'm sure to perish from grief and solitude. My wounds have healed, mainly, but my heart is dead, and my soul a bleeding wound.

I have no memory of how it unfolded. It happened in a blur. It resembled a great explosion, an Armageddon. The colossal destruction wrought here bore a resemblance to a nuclear bomb, or maybe a godsent asteroid. The sun vanished, and day collapsed into night and ushered in absolute darkness. Time ceased to exist. In a blink, the Strip morphed into a dystopian monochrome of its former glory, a gray silhouette of a land that had once existed, a nonplace. In an instant, the place and its people were gone, eerily vanished, swallowed in a swirl of death and darkness. Like a gust of wind, they were gone.

Even the rubble has eerily vanished.

I was standing before the beach, waiting for an omen, when it all unfolded. A black bird was circling overhead, howling sadly, as if trying to whisper something into my ears, but I could not hear it for the waves. I remember there was a great fire, which marched across the ground like a dreadful tornado. A kid with a kite was trying to relocate a bird's nest to safety. It had been flung down from a burning tree and cast into the breakers, its young birds screaming in horror at the downfall. That was my last encounter with a living being. There were no rainbows, and no omens in the sky. Just a kid with a burning kite.

*

All is gone, paradise lost.

All the landmarks that once graced this place are a memory. Goodbye to the sea, our sweet mother, home of the dead, haven of the displaced. In it arc the bodies of my fleeing ancestors who drowned in the tumult of escape. And goodbye to the sad harbor, engulfed in silence, the old hollowed boats anchored at their moorings, tilting with the idle winds of death. The last I saw of it, the bay was roaring with dying breaths, spewing out its dirty bubbles like a rabid dog.

Even the river was murdered in its bed.

Everything looked sad and melancholy, gone and forsaken. The beautiful skies, darkened by the war, deserted by the clouds. The native shores, abandoned by the sea, left to their lonely roars. The old men who taught me how to row against the tide and beat the winds—all dead, mercy on their resting souls. The poor old camp where I lived and loved and sowed my first seeds. The men and women who suffered in silence and died in the dark.

All are gone, goodbye to them, and a pleasant memory.

And I will say one last goodbye, to the mighty Mediterranean, on whose shores I kissed for the first time. I remember it in vivid detail, as if it had happened yesterday. It unfolded rather like a dream, and in many ways it unfolds still. There is a unique taste to the first kiss that can never be replicated, only mooned over and longed for. It's akin to the first sip of coffee, or the first bite of chocolate, or the first puff of tobacco. That kiss never really leaves you. It outlasts memory itself.

My dear old homeland, I will kiss you one last goodbye.

Disheartened, I rest my tired feet on the old seaside rock, the site of memories and desires. O old Mecca of young lovers, I wonder how many romances bloomed and floundered under your feet? I can go no further. I'm worn out, depleted, beaten, overwhelmed with grief and solitude, battered and haunted with ghosts, exhausted with the intensity of my emotions and the burdens of memory. I feel spent, weary, dirty, the dry blood of my war-torn homeland still clinging to my skin. Frail and feeble, and visibly diminished, like the carcass of a tiny bird. Or a skeleton formerly human, flesh and blood. By what unholy miracle I have survived, I can hardly tell.

*

I was rambling the tattered lands without aim, wading my way through wreckage of lost times and spaces, the rubble and ruins of my homeland, when my extraterrestrial friends took pity on me and beamed me away from this doomed place.

I was flying at long last. Some dreams refuse to go unanswered.

Is it my unbridled imagination, or am I still alive? It seems I'm not dead, or resurrected, though I do feel saved. Here, thousands of feet above sea level, I fly fast, safely moored to this flying thing, my godsent spaceship, soaring over the world on this swift-winged angel of death, alive to my good fortune. I smile with existential irony when I realize with delighted surprise that this is the first time I have left the Strip. It takes an extraterrestrial miracle to break the siege. And whether spirited away by my alien friends, or saved by my ancestral spirits, it hardly matters. *Freedom* is all that matters.

*

I sit reveling in my newfound freedom like a bird released from its cage. I look down and see beneath me the last traces of a planet now dead, where nothing stirs but the remains of a warring species that no longer exists. Perhaps if they had known that they would all die in the end, they would have been a little more patient and not too hasty to kill each other. And here, thousands of feet above our sweet Mother Earth, I am halfway through my interstellar journey, perched on the summit of Heaven, enjoying the silent view while Earth drifts away into cosmic slumber, vanishing into the vast blue realms of the cosmos.

I remember my last glimpse of the open sea—a graying vastness of roaring waters, like the afterimage of a bad dream. It bore a sad reflection of the empty landscape, which quickly dwindled away as I climbed up into Heaven, like a fading vision. O sea, grave of the displaced, the site of memories and desires, harbinger of doom.

I remember my last sight of Earth—a sadly diminishing expanse shrinking in the distance like a deflated ball of dirt, a dwindling abyss staring up, yawning. The Strip was nowhere to be seen, for it had been flattened beyond recognition. All was gone. The fruit stands, the candy stores, the perfume shops, the hair salons, the bustling bakeries, the tall minarets, the old churches, the ancient lighthouses, the little boats, the tight alleys, the soup kitchens, the crowded markets, and the people who crowded them were all gone. Everything was gone, save for an orphaned minaret that was still standing, like a miracle, or perhaps like a last witness to the crimes committed there.

It's hard to believe that we had life there once.

*

Imagine my celestial astonishment when I wake up in Heaven and see all the people I have lost in the madness of war gathered here. It seems I have died and been spirited away by my alien friends into this Heaven, which bears an eerie resemblance to the one I imagined, except it's more crowded with children and swollen with refugees.

All are here, well and sound, and eternally happy. The children who were slain in the cradle are wearing wings and flying for fun. Those whose bodies were dismembered by the bombs are given extra wings to fly. All the little ones who were blown into bits are endowed with heavenly wings that never tire or age. The women who died in darkness and grief are dancing in spotless white dresses. The beautiful girl who lost her voice screaming for help is singing sweetly, the memory of the past clearly erased from her mind.

All are here, warm and well. All the orphaned boys and girls who were left behind in the godforsaken jungle, starving, shivering in the cold without so much as a blanket, sit curled before a fireplace whose flames never flicker out. The mother who lost her newborn twins to a bomb is now holding them in an eternal embrace, alive with joy.

Remember the grieving mother who sat cradling a corpse wrapped in a shroud? She's here too, cuddling her baby and lulling her to sleep.

Remember the bewildered child with the princess dress? She's still wearing that dress, though it now looks new and unstained, and is speckled with myriad native flowers. She's wearing a new pair of shoes, and a golden crown to boot. She will grow like a flower and bloom into a beautiful Cinderella. There she sits, in her heavenly kingdom, waving with her golden scepter like a queen happy to reclaim her throne.

All are here, well and sound, and incredibly warm. The mother of nine who stood trembling in the ashen rain pleading for a tent, and the father who lost his family and slept alone amid the ruins, and the parents who stood crying out to the world with a dead child in either arm.

Remember the displaced mother who jettisoned her blanket overboard to unburden the boat, with her newborn still wrapped within? She's here as well, looking happy and sane. All the displaced ones who went under in the madness of escape are resurrected here, the memory of past horrors erased from their minds as if by magic. It amazes me nonetheless that they still remember the good old days.

Remember the little match-seller who froze to death over my grave? She's here too, looking warm and safe, and incredibly beautiful.

*

There is a fitting reward for every innocent soul who perished in darkness and destitution. The children who starved to death are eating chocolate from bending trees, for chocolate is not banned here. The ones who were burned alive, and the ones whose scorched bodies were kept in ice cream trucks, are licking heavenly ice creams that never seem to melt, without an inkling of the tragedy that befell them on Earth. The emaciated children who perished of hunger in the arms of hapless parents are looking healthy and happy, and gaining weight besides. The old man who dwindled into a bearded skeleton is sporting a great belly, whose playful sight seems to amuse the kids.

Wheat and flour abound in plenty. The bread comes out fresh and leavened, whole and unblemished. There are plenty of animal crackers for the children who vomited animal feed and passed out. And for the starved babies who died in the cradle? Rivers of milk and honey.

There are plenty of eggs for the kids, and they come in a rainbow of colors. There's a shiny pile of golden ones for the starved children who died craving a last egg. Kids go egg hunting for fun. They will be astonished to learn that some eggs are made of chocolate too.

Food is plenty, and it comes to you by merely wishing it. There are no hopeless mothers weeping for milk, or hapless fathers fetching food from garbage cans, for there's no garbage in Heaven, as the food here never rots or goes bad—a far cry from wartime food. Water and milk flow from pristine rivers, and fill up your waiting cup as if by magic.

Who knew Heaven was bristling with simple joys!

*

I hear a cacophony of native music and ululations, and I soon gather it's a grand wedding being held for the newly wed couples who were bombed and murdered in their fleeting happiness. The men dance the traditional dance, and the women throw rice on the newlyweds. It's a grand wedding, to judge from the ubiquitous scent of native henna, and native incenses, and native desserts. No food lines.

All are here, basking in the safety of Heaven, reveling in the serenity of eternal peace and infinite calm. The gravediggers, resting at last. The doctors, relaxing idly in the celestial sun. No medicine is needed, for there is no pain. No anesthetics either, for there are no wounds. All pain and wounds are magically healed. The rescuers, resting at long last, taking pleasure in celestial boredom. There's no food dropping, for no place is higher than Heaven. No borders, no crossings, no barriers, no buffer zones, and no walls. No sieges, and no blockades, only open spaces where people roam free. No bombs, only music. No death or mortality. No displacement, and no exile. And no oppression, which I confess might prove boring for a writer, unless you write comedy. For when I meet my uncle, the war photographer, he complains that his photos come out all too perfect. Remember the two old men who played backgammon below amid the rubble? They too complain that whenever they throw the dice, they come out perfectly in their rolls.

The place is too peaceful, eerily quiet in places; no quarrels over clotheslines, for there's no dirt, though the women who fought over the ownership of a clothesline say they miss quarrels. You may go nude if you wish, just be sure to steer away from a certain tree. There are no enemies, only comrades. All are kin, none is a stranger.

Only the devil and his allies on Earth are strangers, for they belong in Hell, with the demons of the deep. There must be one somewhere, for justice's sake!

*

I wave to a group of children wearing wings and flying leisurely. They look slightly different from our children, though from the perspective of Heaven, we all look alike, as equal as the teeth of a comb. There is no ethnic privilege in Heaven. All nations are welcome here; there's a place for everyone, except the murderers, and the warmongers, and the cowards who stood silent at our deaths. Even the poor animals are here—the slain donkeys, and horses, and sheep, and cats, and the brave dogs who chased and howled at enemy soldiers as they slaughtered us. Who said no dogs in Heaven?

Imagine my heavenly delight when I catch a glimpse of my beloved cat, standing in a sea of her kind and gazing at me through her green eyes, shaking her tail to let me know it's time for her milk.

In a playground, I meet my old pals. We say hello and promise to relive the good old days. We reminisce about the good times we had, and the childhood we never had. We have boundless hills and valleys to roam in our timeless leisure. Sadly, there are no dark caves to haunt, or mosquito trucks to chase, but I hear cotton candy carts abound in these quarters, with the same blaring music of yesteryear. And plenty of playgrounds too, not that we are kids anymore, but still it's a small compensation for a lost childhood. For we are still children at heart.

I see a familiar face smiling faintly toward me. I recognize her hennaed hair, and beautiful eyes, and freckled face, and olive skin, and youthful smile that has never aged in my memory. She weeps and falls into my arms, and we agree to marry at last, with a lavish wedding, where food is served in plenty. No bombs or drones, only happy fireworks. We have waited too long, but we have an eternity in which to live and love. We suffered so much on Earth, and now we deserve our heavenly reward. An everlasting honeymoon is awaiting us here.

*

At long last, I locate my father, mother, brothers, and sister—my dear humble people who never knew peace on Earth. We embrace and promise to make up for lost time. Mother looks young and beautiful, as if she were a newlywed. Father looks handsome and dashing. I notice the prayer bump on his forehead has vanished. I hand him his pocket-sized book, and he smiles and says that I can keep it, for there is no praying in Heaven. Mother sits stroking my hair, while my brothers and sister start a playful fight. She wonders what's taken me so long. I'm about to tell her what happened to me down there when she smiles and hands me a familiar book, and says, "Here, I knew you were looking for it." I put the book aside, as I have an eternity to read it, and give her a tight squeeze, feeling safe at last, like I've retreated to the womb.

*

I hear an old familiar voice, deep and earthy. It belongs to my grandmother, who sits curled up by her old millstone, grinding wheat. I see my grandfather, riding his loyal horse through celestial spaces. My displaced ancestors, pitching their permanent tents under the azure sky. All are basking in eternal justice, and eternal happiness, and the joy of eternal return.

What astonishes me the most is that Heaven bears an uncanny resemblance to the native homeland, to judge from the green olive trees and the dear old river, though I do miss the sea. That's how our people wished it, and it was granted. It's paradise lost and found. You can tell from the sight of those native bloody oranges that Heaven is nothing but the dead old homeland resurrected above, away from the surly bounds of Earth. O Heaven, home of the deprived, haven of the oppressed!

My alien friends are nowhere to be found, but I owe them my newfound happiness, though I never had a chance to thank them. People tend to laugh when I mention my extraterrestrial saviors, but I guess you won't believe it until it happens to you.

My loved ones are throwing a party in my honor, but I excuse myself to leave; we will have all of eternity to enjoy together. For now, all I want is fresh air and a quiet place with a homeland view, and an old seaside rock to sit on and rest my tired feet.

# About the Author

**Seraj Assi** is a Palestinian writer living in exile in Washington, DC. *Rubble* is his debut novel.

PM Press is an independent, radical publisher of critically necessary books for our tumultuous times. Our aim is to deliver bold political ideas and vital stories to all walks of life and arm the dreamers to demand the impossible. Founded in 2007 by a small group of people with decades of publishing, media, and organizing experience, we have sold millions of copies of our books, most often one at a time, face to face. We're old enough to know what we're doing and young enough to know what's at stake. Join us to create a better world.

PM Press
PO Box 23912
Oakland CA 94623
510-703-0327
www.pmpress.org

PM Press in Europe
europe@pmpress.org
www.pmpress.org.uk

# FRIENDS OF PM

These are indisputably momentous times—the financial system is melting down globally and the Empire is stumbling. Now more than ever there is a vital need for radical ideas.

In the many years since its founding—and on a mere shoestring—PM Press has risen to the formidable challenge of publishing and distributing knowledge and entertainment for the struggles ahead. With hundreds of releases to date, we have published an impressive and stimulating array of literature, art, music, politics, and culture. Using every available medium, we've succeeded in connecting those hungry for ideas and information to those putting them into practice.

*Friends of PM* allows you to directly help impact, amplify, and revitalize the discourse and actions of radical writers, filmmakers, and artists. It provides us with a stable foundation from which we can build upon our early successes and provides a much-needed subsidy for the materials that can't necessarily pay their own way. You can help make that happen—and receive every new title automatically delivered to your door once a month—by joining as a Friend of PM Press. And, we'll throw in a free T-shirt when you sign up.

Here are your options (each tier receives a 50% discount on all webstore purchases):

- **$30 a month** Get all books and pamphlets
- **$40 a month** Get all PM Press releases (including CDs and DVDs)
  **$100 a month** Superstar—Everything plus PM merchandise and free downloads

For those who can't afford $30 or more a month, we have **Sustainer Rates** at $15, $10, and $5. Sustainers get a free PM Press T-shirt and a 50% discount on all purchases from our website.

Your Visa or Mastercard will be billed once a month, until you tell us to stop. Or until our efforts succeed in bringing the revolution around. Or the financial meltdown of Capital makes plastic redundant. Whichever comes first.